U0874657

YOSHIDA KENKŌ

A Cup of Sake Beneath the Cherry Trees

Translated by
Meredith McKinney

‘It is a most
wonderful
comfort to sit
alone beneath a
lamp, book spread
before you,
and commune
with someone
from the past
whom you have
never met.’

What strange folly, to beguile the tedious hours like this all day before my ink stone, jotting down at random the idle thoughts that cross my mind . . .

*

To be born into this world of ours, it seems, brings with it so much to long for.

The rank of emperor is, of course, unspeakably exalted; even his remotest descendants fill one with awe, having sprung from no mere human seed.

Needless to say, the great ruler, and even the lesser nobles who are granted attendant guards to serve them, are also thoroughly magnificent. Their children and grandchildren too are still impressive, even if they have come down in the world. As for those of lesser degree, although they may make good according to their rank, and put on airs and consider themselves special, they are really quite pathetic.

No one could be less enviable than a monk. Sei

Shōnagon wrote that people treat them like unfeeling lumps of wood, and this is perfectly true. And there is nothing impressive about the way those with power will throw their weight around. As the holy man Sōga, I think, remarked, fame and fortune are an affliction for a monk, and violate the Buddha's teachings.

There is much to admire, though, in a dedicated recluse.

It is most important to present well, in both appearance and bearing. One never tires of spending time with someone whose speech is attractive and pleasing to the ear, and who does not talk overmuch. There is nothing worse than when someone you thought impressive reveals himself as lacking in sensibility. Status and personal appearance are things one is born with, after all, but surely the inner man can always be improved with effort. It is a great shame to see a fine upstanding fellow fall in with low and ugly types who easily run rings round him, and all for want of cultivation and learning.

A man should learn the orthodox literature, write poetry in Chinese as well as Japanese, and study music, and should ideally also be a model to others in his familiarity with ceremonial court customs and precedents. He should write a smooth, fair hand, carry the rhythm well when songs are sung at banquets, and when offered sake, make a show of declining it but nevertheless be able to drink.

*

No matter how splendid in every way, there is something dreadfully lacking in a man who does not pursue the art of love. He is, to coin the old phrase, like a beautiful wine cup that lacks a base.

The elegant thing is for a lover to wander aimlessly hither and yon, drenched with the frosts or dews of night, tormented by fears of his parents' reproaches and the censure of the world, the heart beset with uncertainties, yet for all that sleeping often alone, though always fitfully.

On the other hand, he shouldn't lose himself to love too thoroughly, or gain the reputation of being putty in women's hands.

*

If our life did not fade and vanish like the dews of Adashino's graves or the drifting smoke from Toribe's burning grounds, but lingered on for ever, how little the world would move us. It is the ephemeral nature of things that makes them wonderful.

Among all living creatures, it is man that lives longest. The brief dayfly dies before evening; summer's cicada knows neither spring nor autumn. What a glorious luxury it is to taste life to the full for even a single year. If you constantly regret life's passing, even a thousand long years will seem but the dream of a night.

Why cling to a life which cannot last for ever, only

to arrive at ugly old age? The longer you live, the greater your share of shame. It is most seemly to die before forty at the latest. Once past this age, people develop an urge to mix with others without the least shame at their own unsightliness; they spend their dwindling years fussing adoringly over their children and grandchildren, hoping to live long enough to see them make good in the world. Their greed for the things of this world grows ever deeper, till they lose all ability to be moved by life's pathos, and become really quite disgraceful.

*

Nothing so distracts the human heart as sexual desire. How foolish men's hearts are!

Aroma, for instance, is a mere transient thing, yet a whiff of delightful incense from a woman's robes will always excite a man, though he knows perfectly well that it is just a passing effect of robe-smoking.

The wizard priest of Kume is said to have lost his supernatural powers when he spied the white legs of a woman as she squatted washing clothes. I can quite believe it – after all, the beautiful, plump, glowing flesh of a woman's arm or leg is quite a different matter from some artificial allurement.

*

Beautiful hair on a woman will draw a man's gaze – but we can judge what manner of person she is and the nature of her sensibility even by simply hearing her speak from behind a screen. A mere unintended glimpse of a woman can distract a man's heart; and if a woman sleeps fitfully, and is prepared to endure impossible difficulties heedless of her own well-being, it is all because her mind is on love.

Yes indeed, the ways of love lie deep in us. Many are the allurements of our senses, yet we can distance ourselves from them all. But among them this one alone seems without exception to plague us all, young and old, wise and foolish.

So it is that we have those tales of how a woman's hair can snare and hold even an elephant, or how the rutting stag of autumn will always be drawn by the sound of a flute made from the wood of a woman's shoe.

We must discipline ourselves to be constantly prudent and vigilant lest we fall into this trap.

*

Though a home is of course merely a transient habitation, a place that is set up in beautiful taste to suit its owner is a delightful thing.

Even the moonlight is so much the more moving when it shines into a house where a refined person dwells in tranquil elegance. There is nothing fashionable or showy about the place, it is true, yet the grove of trees is redolent of age, the plants in the carefully untended garden carry a hint of delicate feelings, while the veranda and open-weave fence are tastefully done, and inside the house the casually disposed things have a tranquil, old-fashioned air. It is all most refined.

How ugly and depressing to see a house that has employed a bevy of craftsmen to work everything up to a fine finish, where all the household items set out for proud display are rare and precious foreign or Japanese objects, and where even the plants in the garden are clipped and contorted rather than left to grow as they will. How could anyone live for long in such a place? The merest glimpse will provoke the thought that all this could go up in smoke in an instant.

Yes, on the whole you can tell a great deal about the owner from his home.

The Later Tokudaiji Minister once had rope strung over the roof of the main house to stop the kites from roosting on it. 'What could be wrong with having kites on your roof? This shows what manner of man he is!' exclaimed the poet-monk Saigyō, and it is said he never called there again. I was reminded of this story when I noticed once that Prince Ayanokōji had laid rope over his Kosaka residence. Someone told me, however, that it was because he pitied the frogs in his pond when he observed how crows gathered on the roof to catch them. I was most impressed. Perhaps the Tokudaiji Minister too might have had some such reason for acting as he did?

*

One day in the tenth month, I went to call on someone in a remote mountain village beyond Kurusuno.

Making my way along the mossy path, I came at length to the lonely hut where he lived. There was not a sound except for the soft drip of water from a bamboo pipe buried deep in fallen leaves. The vase on the altar shelf with its haphazard assortment of chrysanthemums and sprigs of autumn leaves bespoke someone's presence.

Moved, I said to myself, 'One could live like this' – but my mood was then somewhat spoiled by noticing at the far end of the garden a large mandarin tree, branches bowed with fruit, that was firmly protected by a stout fence. If only that tree weren't there! I thought.

*

What happiness to sit in intimate conversation with someone of like mind, warmed by candid discussion of the amusing and fleeting ways of this world . . . but such a friend is hard to find, and instead you sit there doing your best to fit in with whatever the other is saying, feeling deeply alone.

There is some pleasure to be had from agreeing with the other in general talk that interests you both, but it's better if he takes a slightly different position from yours. 'No, I can't agree with that,' you'll say to each other combatively, and you'll fall into arguing the matter out. This sort of lively discussion is a pleasant way to pass the idle hours, but in fact most people tend to grumble about things different from oneself, and though you can put up with the usual boring platitudes, such men are far indeed from the true friend after your own heart, and leave you feeling quite forlorn.

*

It is a most wonderful comfort to sit alone beneath a lamp, book spread before you, and commune with someone from the past whom you have never met.

As to books – those moving volumes of *Wenxuan*, the *Wenji* of Bai Juyi, the words of Laozi and *Zhuangzi*. There are many moving works from our own land, too, by scholars of former times.

*

It is an excellent thing to live modestly, shun luxury and wealth and not lust after fame and fortune. Rare has been the wise man who was rich.

In China once there was a man by the name of Xu You, who owned nothing and even drank directly from his cupped hands. Seeing this, someone gave him a 'singing gourd' to use as a cup; he hung it in a tree, but when he heard it singing in the wind one day he threw it away, annoyed by the noise it made, and went back to drinking his water from his hands. What a free, pure spirit!

Sun Chen had no bedclothes to sleep under in the winter months, only a bundle of straw which he slept in at night and put away again each morning.

The Chinese wrote these stories to hand down to later times because they found them so impressive. No one bothers to tell such tales in our country.

*

The changing seasons are moving in every way.

Everyone seems to feel that 'it is above all autumn that moves the heart to tears', and there is some truth in this, yet surely it is spring that stirs the heart more profoundly. Then, birdsong is full of the feel of spring, the plants beneath the hedges bud into leaf in the warm sunlight, the slowly deepening season brings soft mists, while the blossoms at last begin to open, only to meet with ceaseless winds and rain that send them flurrying restlessly to earth. Until the leaves appear on the boughs, the heart is endlessly perturbed.

The scented flowering orange is famously evocative, but it is above all plum blossom that has the power to carry you back to moments of cherished memory. The exquisite kerria, the hazy clusters of wisteria blossom – all these things linger in the heart.

Someone has said that at the time of the Buddha's birthday and the Kamo festival in the fourth month, when the trees are cool with luxuriant new leaf, one is particularly moved by the pathos of things and by a longing for others, and indeed it is true. And who could not be touched to melancholy in the fifth month, when the sweet flag iris leaves are laid on roofs, and the rice seedlings are planted out, and the water rail's knocking call is heard? The sixth month is also moving, with white evening-glory blooming over the walls of poor dwellings, and the smoke from smouldering smudge fires. The purifications of the sixth month are also delightful.

The festival of Tanabata is wonderfully elegant. Indeed so many things happen together in autumn – the nights grow slowly more chill, wild geese come crying over, and when the bush clover begins to yellow the early rice is harvested and hung to dry. The morning after a typhoon has blown through is also delightful.

Writing this, I realize that all this has already been spoken of long ago in *The Tale of Genji* and *The Pillow Book* – but that is no reason not to say it again. After all, things thought but left unsaid only fester inside you. So I let my brush run on like this for my own foolish solace; these pages deserve to be torn up and discarded, after all, and are not something others will ever see.

To continue – the sight of a bare wintry landscape is almost as lovely as autumn. It is delightful to see fallen autumn leaves scattered among the plants by the water's edge, or vapour rising from the garden stream on a morning white with frost. It is also especially moving to observe everyone bustling about at year's end, preparing for the new year. And then there is the forlornly touching sight of the waning moon around the twentieth day, hung in a clear, cold sky, although people consider it too dreary to look at. The Litany of Buddha Names and the Presentation of Tributes are thoroughly moving and magnificent, and in fact all the numerous court ceremonies and events at around this time, taking place as they do amidst the general end-of-year bustle, present an impressive sight. The way the Worship of the Four Directions follows so quickly upon the Great Demon Expulsion is wonderful too.

In the thick darkness of New Year's Eve, people light pine torches and rush about, so fast that their feet virtually skim the ground, making an extraordinary racket for some reason, and knocking on everyone's doors until late at night – but then at last around dawn all grows quiet, and you savour the touching moment of saying farewell to the old year. I was moved to find that in the East they still perform the ritual for dead souls on the night when the dead are said to return, although these days this has ceased to be done in the capital.

And so, watching the new year dawn in the sky, you are stirred by a sense of utter newness, although the sky looks no different from yesterday's. It is also touching to see the happy sight of new year pines gaily decorating the houses all along the main streets.

*

A certain recluse monk once remarked, 'I have relinquished all that ties me to the world, but the one thing that still haunts me is the beauty of the sky.' I can quite see why he would feel this.

*

How mutable the flower of the human heart, a fluttering blossom gone before the breeze's touch – so we recall the bygone years when the heart of another was our close companion, each dear word that stirred us then still unforgotten; and yet, it is the way of things that the beloved should move into worlds beyond our own, a parting far sadder than from the dead. Thus did Mozi grieve over a white thread that the dye would alter for ever, and at the crossroads Yang Zhu lamented the path's parting ways.

In Retired Emperor Horikawa's collection of one hundred poems, we read:

Where once I called on her	*mukashi mishi*
the garden fence is now in ruins –	*imo ga kakine wa*
flowering there I find	*arenikeri*
only wild violets, woven through	*tsubana majiri no*
with rank spring grasses.	*sumire nomi shite*

Such is the desolate scene that once must have met the poet's eye.

*

Nothing is sadder than the aftermath of a death.

How trying it is to be jammed in together in some cramped and inconvenient mountain establishment for the forty-nine-day mourning period, performing the services for the dead. Never have the days passed faster. On the final day everyone is gruff and uncommunicative; each becomes engrossed in the importance of his own tidying and packing, then all go their separate ways. Once home again, the family will face all manner of fresh sorrows.

People go about warning each other of the various things that should be ritually avoided for the sake of the family. What a way to talk, at such a time! Really, what a wretched thing the human heart is!

Even with the passage of time the deceased is in no way forgotten, of course, but 'the dead grow more distant with each day', as the saying goes. And so, for all the memories, it seems our sorrow is no longer as acute as at death, for we begin to chatter idly and laugh again.

The corpse is buried on some deserted mountainside, we visit it only at the prescribed times, and soon moss has covered the grave marker, the grave is buried under fallen leaves, and only the howling evening winds and the moon at night come calling there.

It is all very well while there are those who remember and mourn the dead, but soon they too pass away; the descendants only know of him by hearsay, so they are hardly likely to grieve over his death. Finally, all ceremonies for him cease, no one any longer knows who he was or even his name, and only the grasses of each passing spring grow there to move the sensitive to pity; at length even the graveyard pine that sobbed in stormy winds is cut for firewood before its thousand years are up, the ancient mound is levelled by the plough, and the place becomes a field. The last trace of the grave itself has finally disappeared. It is sad to think of.

*

One morning after a beautiful fall of snow, I had reason to write a letter to an acquaintance, but I omitted to make any mention of the snow. I was delighted when she responded, 'Do you expect me to pay any attention to the words of someone so perverse that he fails to enquire how I find this snowy landscape? What deplorable insensitivity!'

The lady is no longer alive, so I treasure even this trifling memory.

*

Around the twentieth day of the ninth month, someone invited me along to view the moon with him. We wandered and gazed until first light. Along the way, my companion came upon a house he remembered. He had his name announced, and in he went. In the unkempt and dew-drenched garden, a hint of casual incense lingered in the air. It was all movingly redolent of a secluded life.

In due course my companion emerged, but the elegance of the scene led me to stay a little longer and watch from the shadows. Soon the double doors opened a fraction wider; it seemed the lady was gazing at the moon. It would have been very disappointing had she immediately bolted the doors as soon as the visit was over. She could not know that someone would still be watching. Such sensibility could only be the fruit of a habitual attitude of mind.

I heard that this lady died not long after.

*

It is foolish to be in thrall to fame and fortune, engaged in painful striving all your life with never a moment of peace and tranquillity.

Great wealth will drive you to neglect your own well-being in pursuit of it. It is asking for harm and tempting trouble. Though you leave behind at your death a mountain of gold high enough to prop up the North Star itself, it will only cause problems for those who come after you. Nor is there any point in all those pleasures that delight the eyes of fools. Big carriages, fat horses, glittering gold and jewels – any man of sensibility would view such things as gross stupidity. Toss your gold away in the mountains; hurl your jewels into the deep. Only a complete fool is led astray by avarice.

Everyone would like to leave their name unburied for posterity – but the high-born and exalted are not necessarily fine people, surely. A dull, stupid person can be born into a good house, attain high status thanks to opportunity and live in the height of luxury, while many wonderfully wise and saintly men choose to remain in lowly positions, and end their days without ever having met with good fortune. A fierce craving for high status and position is next in folly to the lust for fortune.

We long to leave a name for our exceptional wisdom and sensibility – but when you really think about it, desire for a good reputation is merely revelling in the praise of others. Neither those who praise us nor those who denigrate will remain in the world for long, and others who hear their opinions will be gone in short order as well. Just who should we feel ashamed before, then? Whose is the recognition we should crave? Fame in fact attracts abuse and slander. No, there is nothing to be gained from leaving a lasting name. The lust for fame is the third folly.

Let me now say a few words, however, to those who dedicate themselves to the search for knowledge and the desire for understanding. Knowledge leads to deception; talent and ability only serve to increase earthly desires. Knowledge acquired by listening to others or through study is not true knowledge. So what then should we call knowledge? Right and wrong are simply part of a single continuum. What should we call good? One who is truly wise has no knowledge or virtue, nor honour nor fame. Who then will know of him, and speak of him to others? This is not because he hides his virtue and pretends foolishness – he is beyond all distinctions such as wise and foolish, gain and loss.

I have been speaking of what it is to cling to one's delusions and seek after fame and fortune. All things of this phenomenal world are mere illusion. They are worth neither discussing nor desiring.

*

A certain novice monk in Inaba was rumoured to have a beautiful daughter, and many men came asking for her hand. But the girl ate nothing but chestnuts and never touched grains, so her father declared that she was too eccentric to be marriageable, and rejected them all.

*

When I went to see the horse racing at the Kamo Shrine on the fifth day of the fifth month, the view from our carriage was blocked by a throng of common folk. We all got down and moved towards the fence for a better view, but that area was particularly crowded and we couldn't make our way through.

We then noticed a priest who had climbed a chinaberry tree across the way to sit in its fork and watch from there. He was so sleepy as he clung there that he kept nodding off, and only just managed to start awake in time to save himself from falling each time. Those who saw him couldn't believe their eyes. 'What an extraordinary fool!' they all sneered. 'How can a man who's perched up there so precariously among the branches relax so much that he falls asleep?'

A thought suddenly occurred to me. 'Any of us may die from one instant to the next,' I said, 'and in fact we are far more foolish than this priest – here we are, contentedly watching the world go by, oblivious to death.'

'That's so true,' said those in front of me. 'It's really very stupid, isn't it,' and they turned around and invited me in and made room for me.

Anyone can have this sort of insight, but at that particular moment it came as a shock, which is no doubt why people were so struck by it. Humans are not mere insensate beings like trees or rocks, after all, and on occasion things can really strike home.

*

Those who feel the impulse to pursue the path of enlightenment should immediately take the step, and not defer it while they attend to all the other things on their mind.

If you say to yourself, 'Let's just wait until after this is over,' or 'While I'm at it I'll just see to that,' or 'People will criticize me about such-and-such so I should make sure it's all dealt with and causes no problem later,' or 'There's been time enough so far, after all, and it won't take long just to a wait a little longer while I do this. Let's not rush into things,' one imperative thing after another will occur to detain you. There will be no end to it all, and the day of decision will never come.

In general, I find that reasonably sensitive and intelligent people will pass their whole life without taking the step they know they should. Would anyone with a fire close behind him choose to pause before fleeing? In a matter of life and death, one casts aside shame, abandons riches and runs. Does mortality wait on our choosing? Death comes upon us more swiftly than fire or flood. There is no escaping it. Who at that moment can refuse to part with all they love – aged parents, beloved children, lord and master, or the love of others?

*

The holy man of Shosha had accumulated such merit through recitations of *The Lotus Sutra* that he had attained purity of the Six Senses.

Once, on a journey, he entered the lodging where he was to stay the night and heard the bubbling of a pot of beans being boiled over a fire made from their husks.

'We're so closely related and yet you boil us so brutally!' they were crying, and the bean husks crackling in the flames seemed to him to reply, 'Do you imagine we're boiling you on purpose? It's excruciating for us to be burning like this, heaven knows, but we're powerless to stop. Enough of these recriminations!'

*

As soon as I hear someone's name, I feel I can picture their face, but when I actually meet them no one ever looks as I had been imagining all that time.

Also, I wonder if everyone, on hearing some old tale, imagines it as taking place in a certain part of some house he knows, and identifies the characters with people he sees in life, as I do.

And is it just I who sometimes feels a conviction that what someone is saying, or what you're seeing or thinking just then, has already happened before, though you cannot remember when?

*

Unpleasant things – a great many things cluttering up the area where someone is sitting. A lot of brushes lying on an ink stone. A crowd of Buddhist images in a private worship hall. A large collection of stones and plants in a garden. Too many children and grandchildren in a house.

Too much talk when meeting others. A long list of one's virtuous acts in a supplicatory prayer.

Things that are not unpleasant in large amounts are books on a book cart, and rubbish on a rubbish heap.

*

What kind of man will feel depressed at being idle? There is nothing finer than to be alone with nothing to distract you.

If you follow the ways of the world, your heart will be drawn to its sensual defilements and easily led astray; if you go among people, your words will be guided by others' responses rather than come from the heart. There is nothing firm or stable in a life spent between larking about together and quarrelling, exuberant one moment, aggrieved and resentful the next. You are forever pondering pros and cons, endlessly absorbed in questions of gain and loss. And on top of delusion comes drunkenness, and in that drunkenness you dream.

Scurrying and bustling, heedless and forgetful – such are all men. Even if you do not yet understand the True Way, you can achieve what could be termed temporary happiness at least by removing yourself from outside influences, taking no part in the affairs of the world, calming yourself and stilling the mind. As *The Great Cessation and Insight* says, we must 'break all ties with everyday life, human affairs, the arts and scholarship'.

*

I cannot bear the way people will make it their business to know all the details of some current rumour, even though it has nothing to do with them, and then proceed to pass the story on and do their best to learn more. Wandering monks up from some provincial backwater seem particularly adept at prying into tales about others as if it was their own concern, and spreading the word in such detail that you wonder how on earth they came to know so much.

*

Nor can I bear the way people will spread excited rumours about the latest marvels. A refined person will not learn of things until the rumours are old and stale.

If someone new comes visiting, the boorish and insensitive will always manage to make the visitor feel ignorant by exchanging cryptic remarks about something they all know among themselves, some story or name, chuckling and exchanging knowing glances.

*

When someone complained that it was a great shame the way fine silk covers are so soon damaged, Ton'a replied,

'It is only after the top and bottom edges of the silk have frayed, or when the mother-of-pearl has peeled off the roller, that a scroll is truly impressive' – an astonishingly fine remark, I felt. Similarly, an unmatched set of bound books can be considered unattractive, but Bishop Kōyū impressed me deeply by saying that only a boring man will always want things to match; real quality lies in irregularity – another excellent remark.

In all things, perfect regularity is tasteless. Something left not quite finished is very appealing, a gesture towards the future. Someone told me that even in the construction of the imperial palace, some part is always left uncompleted.

In the Buddhist scriptures and other works written by the great men of old there are also a number of missing sections.

*

The Dainagon Abbot employed a young acolyte by the name of Otozuru-maru, who came to be on intimate terms with one Yasura-dono and was constantly coming and going to visit him.

One day, seeing the lad return, the abbot asked where he had been. 'I've been to see Yasura-dono,' he replied.

'Is this Yasura-dono a layman, or a monk?' enquired the abbot.

Bringing his sleeves together in a polite bow, the acolyte replied, 'I really don't know, sir. I've never seen his head.'

I wonder why not – after all, he would have seen the rest of him.

*

The Yin-Yang masters do not concern themselves with those days of the calendar marked 'Red Tongue Days'. Nor did people of old treat the day as unpropitious. It seems someone more recently has declared it unlucky, and now everyone has begun to avoid it, believing that things undertaken on this day will miscarry. This idea – that whatever is said or done on this day will fail, that objects gained on the day will be lost and plans made will go awry – is ridiculous. If you count the number of failures that happen on an auspicious day, you will find there are just as many.

This is because, in this transient phenomenal world with its constant change, what appears to exist in fact does not. What is begun has no end. Aims go unfulfilled, yet desire is endless. The human heart changes ceaselessly. All things are passing illusion. What is there that remains unchanging? The folly of such beliefs springs from people's inability to understand this.

It is said that evil performed on an auspicious day is always ill-fated, while good performed on an inauspicious one will be blessed by good fortune. It is people who create good fortune and misfortune, not the calendar.

*

A man who was studying archery took two arrows in his hand and stood before the target.

'A beginner should not hold two arrows,' his teacher told him. 'You will be careless with the first, knowing you have a second. You must always be determined to hit the target with the single arrow you shoot, and have no thought beyond this.' With only two arrows, and standing before his master, would he really be inclined to be slapdash with one of them? Yet although he may not have been aware of his own carelessness, his teacher was. The same injunction surely applies in all matters.

A man engaged in Buddhist practice will tell himself at night that there is always the morning, or in the morning will anticipate the night, always intending to make more effort later. And if such are your days, how much less aware must you be of the passing moment's indolence. Why should it be so difficult to carry something out right now when you think of it, to seize the instant?

*

Someone told the following tale. A man sells an ox. The buyer says he will come in the morning to pay and take the beast. But during the night, the ox dies. 'The buyer thus gained, while the seller lost,' he concluded.

But a bystander remarked, 'The owner did indeed lose on the transaction, but he profited greatly in another way. Let me tell you why. Living creatures have no knowledge of the nearness of death. Such was the ox, and such too are we humans. As it happened, the ox died that night; as it happened, the owner lived on. One day's life is more precious than a fortune's worth of money, while an ox's worth weighs no more than a goose feather. One cannot say that a man who gains a fortune while losing a coin or two has made a loss.'

Everyone laughed at this. 'That reasoning doesn't only apply to the owner of the ox,' they scoffed.

The man went on. 'Well then, if people hate death they should love life. Should we not relish each day the joy of survival? Fools forget this – they go striving after other enjoyments, cease to appreciate the fortune they have and risk all to lay their hands on fresh wealth. Their desires are never sated. There is a deep contradiction in failing to enjoy life and yet fearing death when faced with it. It is because they have no fear of death that people fail to enjoy life – no, not that they don't fear it, but rather they forget its nearness. Of course, it must be said that the ultimate gain lies in transcending the relative world with its distinction between life and death.'

At this, everyone jeered more than ever.

*

A lady who had reason to withdraw from the world for a time had retired to a lonely tumbledown house, where she was idling away the long days of her seclusion, when one dimly moonlit evening a certain man decided to call; but as he was creeping stealthily to her door, a dog set up a fierce barking. This brought one of the maidservants. 'Where do you hail from?' she enquired. The man promptly announced himself, and was shown in.

His heart was heavy as he took in his forlorn surroundings. How must she spend her time here? He stood hesitating on the veranda's rough wooden boards. 'This way,' came a wonderfully serene and youthful voice, so he slid open the door with some difficulty and entered.

The place was not so shabby after all, but was modest and refined. At the far end a lamp shone softly, revealing the beauty of the furnishings, and the scent of incense lit some time earlier imbued the place with an evocative and beguiling air.

He heard orders being given among the servants – 'Take care to lock the gate. It may rain. Put the carriage under the shelter of the gate roof' – and talk of where his retainers should spend the night. Then one added, in a soft murmur that nevertheless reached his ears because he was quite close, 'Tonight at least we can sleep easy.'

The two spoke together of all that had happened since

they last met, until the first cock crowed while it was yet night. On they talked earnestly, of matters past and to come, and now the cock's crow was loud and persistent. The day must by now have dawned, he thought, but this was not a place he must hasten to leave before light, so he lingered on a little, until sunlight whitened the cracks in the door. At last, with promises not to forget her, he departed.

Recalling the enchanting scene, he remembers how beautifully green the trees and garden plants glowed in that early summer daybreak, and even now, whenever he passes the house, he turns to gaze until the great camphor tree in the garden is lost to sight.

*

A man famed for his tree-climbing skills once directed another to climb a tall tree and cut branches. While the fellow was precariously balanced aloft, the tree-climber watched without a word, but when he was descending and had reached the height of the eaves the expert called to him, 'Careful how you go! Take care coming down!'

'Why do you say that? He's so far down now that he could leap to the ground from there,' I said.

'Just so,' replied the tree-climber. 'While he's up there among the treacherous branches I need not say a word – his fear is enough to guide him. It's in the easy places that mistakes will always occur.'

Lowly commoner though he was, his words echoed the warnings of the sages.

Apparently one of the laws of kickball also states that if you relax after achieving a difficult kick, this is the moment when the ball will always fall to the ground.

*

There are seven types of people one should not have as a friend.

The first is an exalted and high-ranking person. The second, somebody young. The third, anyone strong and in perfect health. The fourth, a man who loves drink. The fifth, a brave and daring warrior. The sixth, a liar. The seventh, an avaricious man.

The three to choose as friends are – one who gives gifts, a doctor and a wise man.

*

The domestic animals are the horse and the ox. It is a shame to tether the poor things and make them suffer, but it can't be helped, since they are indispensable to us. One should most certainly have a dog, as they are better than men at guarding the house. However, since all the houses around you will have dogs, you probably don't need to go out of your way to get one yourself.

All other creatures, be it bird or beast, are useless.

When you lock an animal that runs free into a cage or chain it up, when you snip the wings of a flying bird and confine it, the beast will ceaselessly pine for the wild and the bird for the clouds. Surely no one with a heart to imagine how unbearable he himself would find it could take pleasure in these creatures' torment. It would take the stony heart of a Jie or a Zhou to enjoy witnessing the suffering of a living creature.

Wang Huizhi loved birds. He watched them frolicking happily in the forest, and made them his companions in his rambles. He did not catch them and make them suffer. We should follow the words of the classic: 'Do not cultivate rare birds or strange beasts in your own land.'

*

Grand Counsellor Masafusa was a fine, scholarly man, and the retired emperor was planning to promote him to Commander of the Guards, when someone in close service informed His Majesty that he had just witnessed something dreadful.

'What was it?' His Majesty enquired.

'I watched through a gap in the fence as Count Masafusa cut off the leg of a live dog to feed to his hawk,' the man replied.

His Majesty was appalled. The thought of Masafusa revolted him, and he was not promoted after all.

It is extraordinary that such a man would own a hawk,

and the story of the dog's leg is absolutely unfounded. The lie was most unfortunate, but how splendid of His Majesty to have reacted with such disgust when he heard the tale.

Overall, it must be said that those who kill or harm living creatures, or set them up to fight each other for their own pleasure, are no better than wild beasts themselves. If you pause and look carefully at the birds and animals, and even the little insects, you will see that they love their children, feel affection for their parents, live in couples, are jealous, angry, full of desire, self-protecting and fearful for their lives, and far more so than men, since they lack all intelligence. Surely one should pity them when they are killed or made to suffer? If you can look on any sentient being without compassion, you are less than human.

*

Yan Hui's firm belief was that he must avoid burdening others. One should not cause suffering and pain to others, nor undermine the will of the humble man.

Some will take pleasure in deceiving, frightening or mocking little children. Adults treat such tales lightly, knowing that they are quite unfounded, but those words will strike deep into the heart of a poor little child, and humiliate, terrify or appal it. It is heartless to enjoy tormenting children in this way.

The joys, angers, sorrows and pleasures of adults too are all based on illusion, but who among us is not attached to the seeming reality of this life?

It harms a man more to wound his heart than to hurt his body. Illness, too, often originates in the mind. Few illnesses come from without. There are times when medicine cannot produce the intended sweat, but shame or fear will always bring one on, which should prove to us that such things come from the mind. We find examples in the classics, after all – think of the man who was hoisted up the Ling Yun Tower to write its signboard, whose hair turned white from fear at the height.

*

Should we look at the spring blossoms only in full flower, or the moon only when cloudless and clear? To long for the moon with the rain before you, or to lie curtained in your room while the spring passes unseen, is yet more poignant and deeply moving. A branch of blossoms on the verge of opening, a garden strewn with fading petals, have more to please the eye. Could poems on the themes of 'Going to view the blossoms to find them already fallen' or 'Written when I was prevented from going to see the flowers' be deemed inferior to 'On seeing the blossoms'? It is natural human feeling to yearn over the falling blossoms and the setting moon – yet some, it seems, are so insensitive that they will declare that since this branch and that have already shed their flowers, there is nothing worth seeing any longer.

In all things, the beginning and end are the most engaging. Does the love of man and woman suggest only their embraces? No, the sorrow of lovers parted before they met, laments over promises betrayed, long lonely nights spent sleepless until dawn, pining thoughts for one in some far place, a woman left sighing over past love in her tumbledown abode – it is these, surely, that embody the romance of love.

Rather than gazing on a clear full moon that shines over a thousand leagues, it is infinitely more moving to see the moon near dawn and after long anticipation, tinged with most beautiful palest blue, a moon glimpsed among cedar branches deep in the mountains, its light now hidden again by the gathering clouds of an autumn shower. The moist glint of moonlight on the glossy leaves of the forest *shii* oak or the white oak pierces the heart, and makes you yearn for the distant capital and a friend of true sensibility to share the moment with you.

Are blossoms and the moon merely things to be gazed at with the eye? No, it brings more contentment and delight to stay inside the house in spring and, there in your bedroom, let your heart go out to the unseen moonlit night.

The man of quality never appears entranced by anything; he savours things with a casual air. Country bumpkins, however, take flamboyant pleasure in everything. They will wriggle their way in through the crowd and stand there endlessly gaping up at the blossoms, sit about under the trees drinking sake and indulging in linked verse-making together and, finally, oafishly break off great branches of blossom to carry away. They will dip their hands and feet into clear spring water, get down to stand in unsullied snow and leave their footprints everywhere, and in short throw themselves into everything with uninhibited glee.

I have observed such people behaving quite astonishingly when they came to see the Kamo festival. Declaring that the procession was horribly late so there was no point in hanging around on the viewing stand, a group retired to a house behind the stands and settled down to eat, drink and play *go* and *sugoroku*, leaving one of their number back on the stand to keep watch. 'It's coming by!' he shouted, whereupon they all leaped frantically to their feet and dashed back, elbowing each other out of the way as they scrambled up, nearly tumbling off in their eagerness to thrust aside the blinds for a better look, jostling for position and craning to miss nothing, and commenting volubly on everything they saw. Then, when that section of the procession had passed, off they went again, declaring they'd be back for the next one. They were clearly only there to see the spectacle.

The upper echelons from the capital, on the other hand, will sit there dozing without so much as a glance at the scene. Young gentlemen of lesser rank are constantly rising to wait on their superiors, while those seated in the back rows never rudely lean forward, and no one goes out of his way to watch as the procession passes.

On the day of the festival everything is elegantly strewn with the emblematic *aoi* leaves, and even before dawn the carriages quietly begin to arrive to secure a good viewing position, everyone intrigued about which carriage is whose, sometimes identifying them by an accompanying servant or ox-boy they recognize. It is endlessly fascinating to watch the carriages come and go, some charming, others more showy. By the time evening draws in, all those rows of carriages and the people who were crammed into the stands have disappeared, and hardly a soul is left. Once the chaos of departing carriages is over, the blinds and matting are taken down from the stands as you watch, and the place is left bare and forlorn, moving you to a poignant sense of the brevity of worldly things. It is this that is the real point of seeing the festival.

Among the people coming and going in front of the stands there are many you recognize, making you realize there are not really so many people in this world. Even if you were destined to die after all these others, clearly your own death cannot be far away. When a large vessel filled with water is pierced with a tiny hole, though each drop is small it will go on relentlessly leaking until soon the vessel is empty. The city is filled with people, but not a day would go by without someone dying. And is it only one or two a day? There are times when the corpses on the pyres of Toribe, Funaoka and elsewhere further afield are piled high, but no day passes without a funeral. And so the coffin sellers no sooner make one than it is sold. Be they young, be they strong, the time of death comes upon all unawares. It is an extraordinary miracle that we have escaped it until now. Can we ever, even briefly, have peace of mind in this world?

It is like the game of *mamakodate*, played with *sugoroku* pieces, in which no one knows which in the line of pieces will be removed next – when the count is made and a piece is taken, the rest seem to have escaped, but the count goes on and more are picked off in turn, so that no piece is finally spared. Soldiers going into battle, aware of the closeness of death, forget their home and their own safety. And it is sheer folly for a man who lives secluded from the world in his lowly hut, spending his days in idle delight in his garden, to pass off such matters as irrelevant to himself. Do you imagine that the enemy Impermanence will not come forcing its way into your peaceful mountain retreat? The recluse faces death as surely as the soldier setting forth to battle.

*

A sensible man will not die leaving valuables behind. A collection of vulgar objects looks bad, while good ones will suggest a futile attachment to worldly things. And it is even more unfortunate to leave behind a vast accumulation. There will be ugly fights over it after your death, with everyone determined to get things for himself. If you plan to leave something to a particular person, you should pass it on while you are still alive.

Some things are necessary for day-to-day living, but one should have nothing else.

*

Even people who seem to lack any finer feelings will sometimes say something impressive.

An alarming-looking ruffian from the eastern provinces once turned to the man beside him and asked if he had any children. 'Not one,' the man replied.

'Well then,' said the Easterner, 'you'll not know what true depth of feeling is. It frightens me to think of a man unacquainted with tenderness. It's having your own children that brings home to you the poignant beauty of life.'

This is indeed true. Without familial love, would such a man as this be able to feel compassion? Even a man who lacks all filial piety will discover how a parent feels when he himself has children.

It is wrong for a man who has taken the tonsure and cast all away to despise those he sees around him encumbered with worldly ties, who go crawling abjectly after this person and that and are full of craving. If you imagined yourself in his place, you would see how he might abase himself so far as to steal for the sake of his beloved parents or wife and children. Rather than seizing thieves and punishing their crimes, it would be better to make the world a place where people did not go hungry or cold. A man without stable means is a man whose heart is unstable. People steal from extremity. There will be no end to crime while the world is not governed well, and men suffer from cold and starvation. It is cruel to make people suffer and drive them to break the law, then treat the poor creatures as criminals.

As for how to improve people's lives, there can be no doubt that it would benefit those below if people in high positions were to cease their luxurious and wasteful ways and instead were kind and tender to the people, and encouraged agriculture. The true criminal must be defined as a man who commits a crime though he is as decently fed and clothed as others.

*

The imperial bodyguard Hada no Shigemi once said of one of the retired emperor's guard, the Shimotsuke Novice Shingan, 'He has the mark of one prone to falling from horses. He should take great care.' Shingan thought this very unlikely, but he did indeed fall from his horse and die. Everyone then decided that the words issuing from such an expert in his field were divinely prophetic.

So just what was this mark? people asked him. 'He

showed all the signs by having a very poor riding seat, and favouring horses that tend to buck,' replied the guard. 'Have I ever been wrong?'

*

It is not good to call on someone if you have no particular reason. Even if you go with some purpose, you should leave promptly once your business is accomplished. It is very annoying if a visit drags on.

There is so much talking when people get together. It is exhausting, disturbs the peace of mind and wastes time better spent on other things. There is nothing to be gained for either party. It is bad, too, to feel irritable as you talk. When you don't care for something, you should come right out and say so.

The exception to all this is when someone after your own heart, whom you feel inclined to talk with, is at a loose end and encourages you to stay a while longer for a peaceful chat. No doubt we all have Ruan Ji's 'welcoming green eyes' from time to time.

It is very nice when a friend simply drops in, has a quiet talk with you, and then leaves. It is also wonderfully pleasing to receive a letter that simply begins, 'I write because it's been some time since I sent news,' or some such.

*

A young man overflows with vigour, things stir his heart, and he is prone to passions. Like a flung ball, such a youth courts danger and physical harm. Riches are wasted in pursuit of magnificence, then all this is suddenly abandoned for the wretched robes of the monk; he is full of fervour and fight, suffers agonies of shame or bitterness, and his fancies are constantly shifting from day to day. He will devote himself to women and pursue infatuations, or take his example from those who have died with no thought to their own safety or longevity, behaving with such reckless daring that 'a long life lies ruined', or let himself be drawn wherever his heart urges, becoming the cause of talk for many years to come. It is indeed in youth that we make our mistakes.

In age, on the other hand, the spirit weakens, we become indifferent and apathetic, and nothing rouses us. The heart grows naturally calm, so that we no longer act in futile ways but instead tend to our bodies, live free of discontent and try to avoid troubling others. Age has more wisdom than youth, just as youth has more beauty than does age.

*

There are many incomprehensible things in this world.

I cannot understand why people will seize any occasion to immediately bring out the sake, delighting in forcing someone else to drink. The other will frown and grimace in painful protest, attempt to throw it away when no one's looking or do his best to escape, but this man will seize him, pin him down and make him swallow cup after cup. A genteel man will quickly be transformed into a madman and start acting the fool; a vigorous, healthy fellow will before your very eyes become shockingly afflicted and fall senseless to the floor. What a thing to do, on a day of celebration! Right into the next day his head hurts, he can't eat, and he lies there groaning with all memory of the previous day gone as if it were a former life. He neglects essential duties both public and private, with disastrous effects. It is both boorish and cruel to subject someone to this sort of misery. Surely a man who has had this bitter experience will be filled with regret and loathing. Anyone from a land that lacked this custom would be amazed and appalled to hear of its existence in another country.

It is depressing enough just to witness this happening to another. A man who had always seemed thoughtful and refined will burst into mindless laughter, prattle on and on, his lacquered court cap askew, the ties of his robes loosened and the skirts hauled up above his shins, and generally behave so obliviously that he seems a changed man. A woman will blatantly push her hair up away from her face, throw back her head and laugh quite shamelessly, and seize the hand of the person with the sake, while the more uncouth might grab one of the snacks and hold it to someone else's mouth or eat it herself – a quite disgraceful sight. People bellow at the top of their lungs, everyone sings and prances about, and an old monk is called in, who proceeds to bare his filthy black shoulder and writhe about so that you can hardly stand to watch, and you loathe just as much the others who sit there enjoying the spectacle.

Some will make you cringe by the way they sing their own praises, others will cry into their drink, while the lower orders abuse each other and get into quite shocking and appalling fights. Finally, after all manner of disgraceful and pitiful behaviour, the drunkard will seize things without permission, then end up hurting himself by rolling off the veranda or tumbling from his horse or carriage. If he's of a class that goes on foot he'll stagger away down the high road, doing unspeakable things against people's walls or gates as he goes. It is quite disgusting to see the old monk in his black robe stumbling off, steadying himself with his hand on the shoulder of the lad beside him and rambling on incomprehensibly.

If drinking like this profited us in this world or the next, what could one say? But in this world it leads to all manner of error, and causes both illness and loss of wealth. Wine has been called 'the greatest of medicines', but in fact all sickness springs from it. It is claimed that you forget your sorrows in drink, but from what I can see, men in their cups will in fact weep to recall their past unhappiness. As for the next world – having lost the wisdom you were born with, reduced all your good karma to ashes, built up a store of wickedness and broken all the Buddhist precepts, you are destined for hell. Remember, the Buddha teaches that those who lift the wine glass either to their own lips or to others' will spend five hundred lifetimes without hands.

Yet, loathsome though one finds it, there are situations when a cup of sake is hard to resist. On a moonlit night, a snowy morning, or beneath the flowering cherry trees, it increases all the pleasures of the moment to bring out the sake cups and settle down to talk serenely together over a drink. It is also a great comfort to have a drink together if an unexpected friend calls round when time is hanging heavy on your hands. And it is quite wonderful when sake and snacks are elegantly served from behind her curtains by some remote and exalted lady.

It is also quite delightful to sit across from a close friend in some cosy little nook in winter, roasting food over the coals and drinking lots of sake together. And delightful too on a journey to sit about on the grass together in some wayside hut or out in the wild, drinking and lamenting the lack of a suitable snack. And it's a fine thing when someone who really hates having sake pressed on them is forced to have just a little. You are thrilled when some grand person singles you out and offers to refill your cup, urging, 'Do have more. You've barely drunk.' And it is also very pleasing when someone you would like to get to know better is a drinker and becomes very pally with you in his cups.

All things considered, a drunkard is so entertaining he can be forgiven his sins. Think of the charming scene when a master throws open the door on his servant, who is sound asleep next morning after an exhausting night on the drink. The poor befuddled fellow rushes off, rubbing his bleary eyes, topknot exposed on his hatless head, only half dressed and clutching the rest of his trailing clothes, his hairy shins sticking out below his lifted skirts as he scampers into the distance – a typical drunk.

*

The one thing a man should not have is a wife.

One is impressed to hear that a certain man always lives alone, while someone who is reported to have married into this or that family, or to have taken a wife and be living together, will find himself quite looked down on. 'He must have married that nondescript girl because he thought she was something special,' people will say scornfully, or if she is a good woman they will think, 'He'll be so besotted that he treats her like his own personal buddha.' The impression is even more dreary when she runs the house well. It is depressing to watch her bear children and fuss over them, and things don't end with his death, for then you have the shameful sight of her growing old and decrepit as a nun.

No matter who the woman may be, you would grow to hate her if you lived with her and saw her day in day out, and the woman must become dissatisfied too. But if you lived separately and sometimes visited her, your feelings for each other would surely remain unchanged through the years. It keeps the relationship fresh to just drop in from time to time on impulse and spend the night.

*

What a shame it is to hear someone declare that things lose their beauty at night! All lustre, ornamentation and brilliance come into their own at night.

In daylight, one can keep things simple and dress sedately. But the best clothing for night is showy and dazzling formal wear. The same goes for people – a good-looking person will look still finer by lamplight, and it's charming to hear a careful voice speaking in darkness. Scents and music too are still lovelier at night.

It is a fine thing to see a man who calls on some great household looking his best late on an uneventful evening. Young people who pay attention to such things will always notice one's appearance no matter what the hour, so it is wise to dress well whatever the situation, whether formal or informal, and most especially at times when one is inclined to relax and unwind. Particularly delightful is when a fine gentleman has bothered to plaster down his hair though it is after dark, or when a lady slips from the room late at night to take up a mirror and see to her face before rejoining the company.

*

When the now-deceased Tokudaiji Minister of the Right was Superintendent of Police, he was one day holding court at his central gate when the ox of one of the officers, Akikane, broke loose, got into the court room, scrambled up on to the Superintendent's seating platform and there settled down to chew its cud. This was deemed a disturbingly untoward event, and everyone present declared that the beast should be taken off for Yin-Yang divination to determine the meaning.

However, when the Superintendent's father the Minister heard of this, he declared, 'An ox has no understanding. It has its four legs which can take it anywhere. There is no reason to impound a skinny beast that happens to have brought some lowly official here.' He had the ox returned to its master, and changed the matting where the ox had lain. There were no ill consequences from the event.

It is sometimes said that if you see something sinister and choose to treat it as normal, you will thereby avert whatever it portended.

*

Nothing in this world can be trusted. Fools put all their faith in things, and so become angry and bitter.

The powerful should place no faith in their powerful

position. The strong are the first to go. The rich should never depend on their wealth. A fortune can easily disappear from one moment to the next. A scholar should never be complacent about his skills. Even Confucius did not meet with the reception he deserved. The virtuous should not rely on their virtue. Even the exemplary Yan Hui met with misfortune. Nor should those favoured by the emperor be smug. You may at any time find yourself instead faced with execution for some crime. Never rely on your servants to be loyal. They can rebel and flee. Never put your faith in others' goodwill. They will inevitably change their minds. Never depend on a promise made. People seldom keep their word.

If you rely neither on yourself nor on others, you will rejoice when things go well, and not be aggrieved when they don't. Maintain a clear space on either side, and nothing will obstruct you; keep open before and behind you, and you will be unimpeded. If you let yourself be hemmed in, you can be squeezed to breaking point. Without care and flexibility in your dealings with the world, you will find yourself in conflict and be damaged, while if you live calmly and serenely, not a hair on your head will come to harm.

Humans are the most miraculous and exalted of all things in heaven and earth. And heaven and earth are boundless. How, then, could we differ in essence? If our spirit is open and boundless, neither fear nor joy will obstruct it, and we will remain untroubled by the world.

*

There is a place in Tamba called Izumo, where the deity of the great Izumo Shrine has been installed in a magnificent shrine building. The area is ruled by a certain Shida, who one autumn invited a great many people, including the holy man Shōkai. 'Come and pray to Izumo,' he said, 'and let us feast on rice cakes.' He led them to the shrine, and every one of them prayed and was filled with faith.

The holy man was immensely moved by the sight of the guardian Chinese lion and Korean dog, which were placed back to back and facing backwards. 'How marvellous!' he exclaimed, close to tears. 'Such an unusual position to stand them in! There must be some deep reason behind it.' Then he turned to the others. 'How can you not have noticed this wonder?' he cried. 'I'm amazed at you.'

They were very struck. 'Yes indeed,' they all declared, 'they *are* different from elsewhere. We'll tell this to everyone back in the capital.'

The holy man now wished to learn more, so he called over an elderly and wise-looking shrine priest. 'There must be some interesting tale explaining the placement of these images,' he said. 'Do be so kind as to tell us.'

'Indeed there is,' replied the priest. 'Some naughty children did it. A disgraceful business,' and so saying he went over to the statues, set them to rights and walked off.

The holy man's tears of delight had been for nothing.

*

He whose deep love spurs him to dare all and go to his beloved, though 'watchful eyes surround the stealthy lover' and 'guards are set to snare him in the dark', will leave them both replete with powerful memories of all the moments when they tasted life's poignancy to the full. It must feel very awkward and unromantic for the woman, however, if a man simply takes her as his wife with the full consent of the family and without further ado.

How dreary it is when a woman hard up in the world announces that she will 'answer the call of any current' so long as he is well-off, be it some unsuitable old priest or an uncouth Easterner, and a go-between sets about singing the praises of each to the other, with the result that she comes to someone's house as a bride without either knowing the other at all. What on earth would they say to each other when they first come face to face? On the other hand, a couple can find endless conversation in the memories of long hardships overcome, 'forging their way through the dense autumn woods' to be together at last.

It can generally be said that a great deal of dissatisfaction results from a marriage set up by a third party. If the wife is excellent and the man a lowly and ugly old fellow, he will despise her for allowing herself to be thrown away on the likes of himself, and feel ashamed in her presence – a deplorable situation.

If you can never linger beneath the clouded moon on

a plum-scented evening, nor find yourself recalling the dawns when you made your way home through the dew-soaked grasses by her gate after a night of love, you had best not aspire to be a lover at all.

*

The full moon's perfect roundness lasts barely a moment, and in no time is lost. Those with no eye for such things, it seems, fail to see how it changes in the course of a night.

An illness will grow graver as each moment passes, and death is already close at hand, yet while the sickness is still mild and you are not yet confronting death, you are lulled by your accustomed assumptions of a normal life in an unchanging world, and choose to wait until you have accomplished all you want in life before calmly turning your thoughts to salvation and a Buddhist practice, with the result that when you fall ill and confront death, none of your dreams has been fulfilled. Now, too late, you repent of your long years of negligence, and swear that if only you were to recover you would dedicate yourself unstintingly day and night to this thing and that – but for all your prayers your illness grows graver, until you lose your senses and die a raving death. It happens to so many of us. We must fully grasp this, here and now.

If you plan to turn your thoughts to the Buddhist Way after you have fulfilled all your desires, you will find that those desires are endless. What could be achieved, in this illusory life of ours? All desire is delusion. If desires arise within you, realize that they spring from your lost and deluded mind, and ignore them all. Relinquish all today and turn to the Buddhist path, and you will be freed of all obstruction, released from the need for action, and lasting peace will be yours body and soul.

*

The year I turned eight, I asked my father, 'What sort of thing is a buddha?'

'A buddha is what a human becomes,' he replied.

'How does a human become a buddha?' I asked.

'You become a buddha by following the Buddha's teaching,' he answered.

'So who taught the Buddha?' I asked.

'He became a buddha by following the teaching of previous buddhas,' he said.

'So what sort of buddha was the first one who began the teaching?' I asked.

My father laughed and replied, 'I suppose he just fell from the sky like rain or rose out of the earth like water.'

He used to enjoy recounting this story to others, adding, 'He had me cornered. I couldn't think what to reply.'

PENGUIN

LITTLE BLACK

CLASSICS

PENGUIN

LITTLE BLACK

CLASSICS

PENGUIN

LITTLE BLACK

CLASSICS

Penguin Little Black Classics Vol. I

01. GIOVANNI BOCCACCIO
Mrs Rosie and the Priest

02. EDGAR ALLAN POE
The Tell-Tale Heart

03. ANTON CHEKHOV
Gooseberries

04. LEO TOLSTOY
How Much Land Does a Man Need?

05. GUSTAVE FLAUBERT
A Simple Heart

06. RYUNOSUKE AKUTAGAWA
The Life of a Stupid Man

07. THOMAS HARDY
The Withered Arm

08. KENKO
A Cup of Sake Beneath the Cherry Trees

09. WILLIAM BLAKE
Tyger Tyger

10. RAINER MARIA RILKE
Letters to a Young Poet

“在孤灯下独坐翻书，
与古人相伴，
真是乐何如哉！”

PENGUIN

LITTLE BLACK

CLASSICS

*此中文译本译自日语原文

樱花树下的清酒

A Cup of Sake Beneath the Cherry Trees

［日］吉田兼好 著

文东 译

中信出版集团 · 北京

图书在版编目（CIP）数据

企鹅经典·小黑书. 第一辑：英、汉 / (日) 吉田兼好等著；文东等译. -- 北京：中信出版社，2018.11（2022.7 重印）
书名原文：Penguin Little Black Classics
ISBN 978-7-5086-9400-9

Ⅰ. ①企… Ⅱ. ①吉… ②文… Ⅲ. ①世界文学—作品综合集—英、汉 Ⅳ. ①I11

中国版本图书馆 CIP 数据核字 (2018) 第 193780 号

A Cup of Sake Beneath the Cherry Trees
Selection taken from Essays in Idleness (Tsurezuregusa), which was probably written around 1329–31. This selection published in Penguin Classics 2015. Translation copyright © Jay Rubin, 2006. The moral right of the translator has been asserted.
Simplified Chinese translation copyright © 文东. All rights reserved.

本书仅限中国大陆地区发行销售

® "企鹅"及其相关标识是企鹅图书有限公司已经注册或尚未注册的商标。
未经允许，不得擅用。
封底凡无企鹅防伪标识者均属未经授权之非法版本。

企鹅经典：小黑书　第一辑
樱花树下的清酒

著　　者：[日] 吉田兼好
译　　者：文东
出版发行：中信出版集团股份有限公司
（北京市朝阳区惠新东街甲 4 号富盛大厦 2 座 邮编 100029）
承 印 者：河北鹏润印刷有限公司

开　　本：787mm×1092mm　1/32　　印　　张：41　　字　　数：300 千字
版　　次：2018 年 11 月第 1 版　　印　　次：2022 年 7 月第 13 次印刷
京权图字：01-2018-6477
书　　号：ISBN 978-7-5086-9400-9
定　　价：149.00 元（全 10 册）

版权所有·侵权必究
如有印刷、装订问题，本公司负责调换。
服务热线：400-600-8099
投稿邮箱：author@citicpub.com

序段

无聊之日，枯坐砚前，心中不由得杂想纷呈，乃随手写来；其间似有不近常理者，视为怪谈可也。

*

人生在世，最是贪图名位。

天皇固然尊贵至极，皇亲国戚也都是金枝玉叶，不是寻常人可以高攀；摄政关白[1]在一人之下、万人之上，当然不容奢望。

1. 摄政是指在天皇年幼时，帮助处理国政的大臣官职，关白则是在天皇成年后，帮助处理国政的大臣官职。此处意指一人担任了两种职务，也可简称为“摄关”。（说明：书中脚注除特别标明的之外，均为编者注。）

至于身在大内，号称“舍人”的诸贵人，也不能等闲视之。其子孙即便破落，也自有其清姿贵格。相比之下，有一点身份就小人得志、自命不凡的人，就不足道了。

世上怕没有多少人把法师瞧得上眼吧。清少纳言就说过：人视之“犹如木屑”。说得很客观。法师一辈子高座说法，俯临众生，似有无上的权威，但对他来说，究竟有什么意义呢？增贺上人似乎说过，一心求名，是有违佛陀教义的。

不过真心舍弃现世、皈依佛门的人，倒颇为令人钦羡。

人都想有秀美的姿容。不过谈吐招人喜爱而并不多话的人，也让人整天面对都不觉得乏味。姿采虽然炫目，德行并不相符的人，就着实令人惋惜了。德行与容貌都是天生的，姑且不论。思想境界，通过持续不断的修习，能够日复一日地精进。天生容貌气质不错的人，如果腹中并无才学，又常与品貌俱无的人在一起，甚至被其习性品味所浸染，比他们还不如，就实在是我所不愿看到的。

我对于世上男子的期许，在于有修身齐家的真才实学，长于诗赋文章，通晓和歌乐理，精通典章制度，而

能够为人表率，这是最理想的。其次，工于书法，信笔挥洒皆成模样；善于歌咏，而能合乎音律节拍；对于席上别人的劝酒，如果推辞不了，也能略饮一点，以不伤应酬的和气，对于男人来说，这也是相当好的事。

事事能干却不解风情的男子，好比没有杯底的玉杯，中看不中用。

相比之下，彷徨无计、流离失所，整日里晨霜夜露、疲于奔命，既怕听父母的训诫，又担心世人的讥讽，时时刻刻心中慌乱不安，而常常孤枕难眠，这样的日子，倒是其味无穷。

只要不一味沉迷于女色，且让女子们知道自己不是随意苟且之人，就比较得体了。

*

倘若无常野的露水和鸟部山的云烟都永不消散，世上的人，既不会老，也不会死，则纵然有大千世界，又哪里有生的情趣可言呢？世上的万物，原本是变动不居、生死相续的，也唯有如此，才妙不可言。

天生万物，而以人之寿命最长。其他如蜉蝣，早上

出生晚上即死；如夏蝉，只活一夏而不知有春与秋。然而抱着从容恬淡的心态过日子，一年都显得漫长无尽；抱着贪婪执着的心态过日子，纵有千年也短暂如一夜之梦。

以过客之身，暂居于世上，等待老丑之年的必然到来，到底所图为何呢？寿则多辱。所以至迟四十岁以前，就应该瞑目谢世，这是天大好事。过了这个年纪，还没有自惭形秽的觉悟，仍然热衷于在众人中抛头露脸，等到了晚年，又溺爱子孙，奢望在有生之年看到他们功成名就，把心思一味地放在世俗的名利上，对人情物趣一无所知，这样的人，想起来就觉得可悲可厌。

*

世上最能迷惑人心的，莫过于色欲。人心实在是愚昧啊！

明知薰香并不能常驻，虽暂时附着于衣物之上，闻着也不禁心旌荡漾，难以自持。

昔年有位久米仙人，能够御空而行。当他飞过家乡时，看见河边洗衣女用双脚踏踩衣物，裸露出雪白的小

腿，心中起了色欲，顿时丧失神通之力，从天上掉了下来。不过女人手足的丰满美艳如凝脂，是其天然的本色，能够让人心迷惑，倒在情理之中。

女子美发的修饰，最引人注目。至于她的人品、气质之类，就算隔帘相语，不睹其面，也能从二三语中听出大概来。女人的作为，能让男人心旌荡漾、神魂颠倒。她自己也常为春思所催，不能安眠，以至于不惜自荐于枕席之间，行苟且之事。这都是心怀色欲的缘故。

人心的爱欲，根自本性，其源也远。能令人沾惹六尘的嗜欲虽然不少，舍而弃之，是可以办到的。唯有爱欲，不论老幼贤愚，莫不为其所惑，不能了断。

是以用女人的发丝搓为绳索，能够拴住象腿不令其动；以女人的木屐削而为笛，横吹之声能令秋日之牡鹿集于眼前。

想来这色欲之惑，是最需戒惧的。

*

住所要舒适自在，虽说浮生如逆旅，也不妨有盎然的意趣。

高人雅士幽居之所，月光流入时，自有一股沁人心脾的气象。今天的时尚，追逐的都是些恶俗的风格，一无可取。此间则是古木缭绕、园草杂生，一派天然野趣。篱围与墙垣的造设，要考虑到周边的景致宜人，日常器物的措置，也一定富有古朴之趣，没有一丝做作的痕迹，才可以让人到此则雅兴勃发。

唐土与日本之器物，有极精致的，都是工匠们费尽心思、百般雕琢而成，如果将它们错杂并陈，又将庭前的草木，一律违拗其天性，肆意摧残，看了真让人心生厌恶。这样的地方，又怎么能长住呢？我每见到这样的庭户，就想，搞得这么精致，谁知道它哪天不会顷刻间付诸一炬呢？

大体说来，从住所的布置情况，就能够推断主人的品位气质。

后德大寺大臣[1]在寝殿中拉了绳索，不让野鸢飞到庭院中来。前来造访的西行法师看见了，就问："就算野鸢飞进来，又有什么关系？这位大人怎么会有这样的心胸呢？"据说他从此以后再不来这里了。绫小路宫居住的

1. 此处指的应是后德大寺左大臣藤原实定。他的祖父因修建德大寺而被称为"德大寺左大臣"。

小坂殿的梁柱上，也曾经拉了绳，我因此才想起西行法师的事。小坂殿中的人说：“这是因为乌鸦飞进来啄食池中的青蛙，亲王心痛那些青蛙的缘故。”如果是这样的话，就是一件大好事了。后德大寺大臣那么做，或者也有他的原因吧，只是我不知道而已。

*

神无月时节[1]，我路过叫栗栖野的地方，到一个山村去。

沿着长满苔藓的小路走了很久，来到山村的深处，见到一个清寂的佛庵。被落叶所埋的引水筒中，水声泠泠可闻，此外便寂然无声。在于伽棚上，看到散放着摘下的菊花、红叶，才知道此处仍有人居住。

如此简陋的地方，也有人居住，不禁感慨系之。又见前方庭园里，有一株果实沉沉的橘树，只是四周严实地围着一圈篱栅，有些令人扫兴。如果没有这棵树，这里的天然之趣，或者就得以保全了吧？

---

1. 日本民间将一年划分为十二个月，相当于我们的农历节气，神无月对应的是农历十月。

*

与志趣相投的友人从容闲谈，不论所谈为饶有趣味之事，还是琐屑无聊之事，都能以性情相见，真是一大快乐。不过这样的人很难遇到。如果谈话的对象，意见与自己一味相同，则与自己独坐有何差异？

我辈倾谈之时，有完全倾向于对方意见的，也有意见略有分歧的，要争论起来，说“我的看法不是这样”“因此我的结论是”等等，在闲来无事时，都挺有意思的。有人对世道人心颇为不满，而我的想法则迥然不同，与之论辩一番，也可稍慰寂寥之心。然而毕竟心存隔阂，不能尽兴，和与知己晤对时的感觉不同。

*

在孤灯下独坐翻书，与古人相伴，真是乐何如哉！

书籍当中，《文选》的各卷都是富于情趣的作品，除此之外，如白居易的《白氏文集》、老子《道德经》及庄子《南华真经》等，都是佳作。本国历代诸博士的著述

中，也常有高妙之作。

*

人如果立身简素，不慕豪奢，不敛财货，不贪图功名利禄，则可谓人中之上品也。自古以来，很少见到富贵贤人。

唐土有个许由，没有任何身外之物。有人见他用双手捧水喝，就送他一个水瓢。他将水瓢挂在树上，因为风吹得响动，听了心烦，就弃而不用，仍然用手捧水喝。此人心中，何其清澈啊！

还有个名叫孙晨的人，冬天没有被褥，只有蒿草一束，晚上睡在上面，早上便收起来。

唐土的人视之为高士，记入书中传之后世。此等之人若在我国，是无人记述的。

*

万物随四季的更替，各有其不同的情趣。

人都说，秋天的事物最有情趣。这话确乎不错。然而

最使人心潮涌动的则莫过于春色。当此之际，啁啾鸟鸣中饱含春意，和煦的阳光下，幼草在墙根悄然萌动，而春意随之渐浓。此时霞光遍洒，众花含苞欲放，如不幸遇上连日风雨，则又仓皇殒落、飘散一地。此后则草木繁滋、天地转绿，其中触动人心、惹人愁思的，就多了。

橘之花，本就令人怀旧了；梅之香，也让人思虑往昔，牵惹旧情；何况还有棣棠之花的艳光明丽，藤花的娇弱无依、我见犹怜。凡此种种，都令人逡巡流连，不能忘怀。

浴佛日与祭祀日的时候，到处装饰着葵花，初发的新叶与嫩枝，透出欣欣的生意，让人有清凉之感。于是有人说，这是人世间的情趣与人的恋世之心最为浓郁的时候，此话不假。五月间，要在门上插菖蒲驱邪，稻田里开始插稻秧，水鸡的鸣叫笃笃如叩门之声，都让人为之心动。六月里，穷人家的墙根开满了白色的夕颜花，到处燃起驱赶蚊虫的烟火，很有味道。六月末的大祓[1]也很有意思。

---

1. 大祓即大祓式，每年日本各大神社都会举行两次的祭祀仪式。一次在夏越晦日，另一次在大晦日（过年之祓）。夏越大祓旨在将上半年积累的晦气和过错清除，平安的迎来下半年，也顺利度过容易生病的夏季。

七夕的祭仪很是优雅。夜晚逐渐转凉，大雁飞来，在天际鸣叫，芦荻之叶开始变黄，早稻收割、晾晒等事务接踵而来。秋日，乃是农事最多的时节。劲风吹拂的晚秋之晨，也有趣。这样的情景，在《源氏物语》《枕草子》等书中都有过描述，然而相同的事物，亲身经历后，不妨自己也来描述一番。心中有所感触而不把它表达出来，不免会腹胀气闷，郁积不堪，所以就信手写下来。不过也没有必要拿给别人看，随手扔掉就是了。

冬日草木枯萎的景色，不下于秋色。早上起来，水边的草地上，散落着红叶，泛着白色的霜气；庭院的流水之上，寒烟缭绕，颇饶意趣。就要到年终了，看着世人忙着备置货物，心中也不免有所感触。

过腊月二十日后，月亮就见不着了，静夜里面没有什么可观赏的，只有一天的澄澈清寒，令人有寂寞之感。佛名会、祭陵使诸事都很有意趣，也让人心怀崇敬。这个时候，朝中政事繁忙，又要为新春到来时的诸事务做好准备，还真不轻松。除夕夜宫中的追傩仪式与紧接着元日早上皇上的四方拜仪式，都非常有意思。

除夕，众人于午夜前手持松枝火把狂呼乱叫，四处叩门，奔跑起来好像双脚都没有着地，哪知道为了什么

呢。天亮之后，到处寂静无声，只有旧年的余味在心头萦回，令人有怅然之感。除夕之夜原本是祭奠亡灵的时间，但现在京城已经没有这个风俗了，只在关东地区还有人这么做。这也是个让人产生兴趣的事。

元日的早晨，晴空万里，景色与昨日并无两样，但心情却大不相同，真是奇怪。京城里，通衢大道的两旁，家家户户都摆出了门松，一眼望去，绵延不绝，充满盎然的生机，令人心生喜爱，真是有味道啊。

*

有遁世者说："我在世上已经了无牵挂，只对于时序节令的推移，还不能忘怀。"此话我深以为然。

*

人心是不待风吹而自落的花。以前的恋人，还记得她情深意切的话，但人已离我而去，形同路人。此种生离之痛，有甚于死别也。故见到染丝，有人会伤心；面对岔路，有人会悲泣。堀川院的百首和歌中有歌云：

旧垣今又来，
彼姝安在哉？
唯见萋萋处，
寂寞堇花开。

这种寂寞的景况，谁说没有呢。

*

死后的情景，是最令人伤心的。

死后中阴期间，遗体停在山寺里，亲戚朋友从各处云集而来，举行法事。一时间这里就显得拥挤嘈杂，让人心绪不宁。时间过得很快，不觉就是最后一天了，大家都意兴阑珊，彼此之间也没什么话说了，于是收拾行李，各自返回来处。回家之后，让人伤心的事恐怕会更多吧。

有人说：“这种事不要随便谈论，多考虑下活着的人吧。”这世道竟然有这样的言论，想起来真让人感到遗憾。

对亡人的追思，并不随岁月的流逝而消减，但古话说“去者日以疏”，其哀伤之情，已不如当初深切，乃至说起往事时，已是言笑如常。

遗骸葬于了无人迹的深山之中，只有在忌日才去洒扫一次。不久，坟上的碑碣便长出青苔，落叶也覆盖了墓地，来访的，只有日暮的风、夜半的月罢了。

怀念者在世时尚且如此，当其逝世之后，子孙只是听说其人，又如何会有由衷的缅怀呢？从此墓地就再无人凭吊，沦为无名荒坟，只有年年春草，令善感者望之动情。呜咽之苍松，不待千年就已伐而为薪，古墓也犁为田地，从此再无形迹可寻，可悲啊！

*

早晨起来，白雪飞舞，真是意趣盎然。又因有事要告诉某人，就去了一封信，信中只字没有提到早晨的飞雪。对方回信说：“对这场雪作何感想，尊驾真是吝于一言。如此俗物，岂能与我言事？君胸中甚少情趣也。”这话着实令人回味。

这位友人如今已经故去，但这件小事，却令我难忘。

*

九月二十日，应某人的邀约，一起去赏月夜游。中途此人一时兴起，要去拜访他的一位友人。于是派人传达入内，我则站在荒芜的庭院中等他。四下里露气繁重，飘浮着薰香的气味，这幽居的住所，景致还不错。

那人不久便从屋里出来，我还在欣赏美景。从暗处望去，见主人送完客后，又把旁边的窗户推开一点，抬头望月。此时如果只是关门进屋，就毫无韵味了。她却不知道外面有人看到她推户赏月，所以此举当出于她平素的修养，绝不是做给人看的。

听说此主人不久即去世了。

*

被名利驱使，一辈子紧张劳累，是何等不明智的事啊!

只顾积累钱财，忽略了修身养性，钱财就只是招累买烦的东西。而“身后堆金拄北斗”，又把烦恼都留给了后人。凡夫俗子们就喜欢看到家中堆金砌银，十分无聊。

乘高车、坐大马，穿金戴玉，在明白人看来，不仅讨厌，而且愚不可及。最好还是“捐金于山，沉珠于渊”。一味沉迷于利欲的人，可谓愚蠢之至。

人都想有不朽的盛名能够传诸后世。达官贵人，不一定都是忠贞正直的人。名门之下，也有拙劣之辈，靠出身和运气跻身庙堂，甚至过着穷奢极欲的生活。相反，杰出的圣贤，一生地位卑下、怀才不遇的，也不乏其人。因此，一心渴慕高官显位的人，其愚蠢的程度，仅次于沉醉利欲的人。

还有想以出众的智慧与品行留名后世的人。然而这也是经不起推敲的：一般喜爱名誉的人，都喜欢听到世人的赞扬。只是不管是赞扬你的人，还是诋毁你的人，在世上都待不久，替你传名的人，也要不多久就消逝了。害怕愧对谁，希望得到谁的认可，又有什么意义呢？非议随声誉而起，身后之名毫无用处，执意去追求，实在也是愚蠢之举。

一心想变得智慧或者成为贤者的人，要知道虚伪出自智慧，一身才能让人一生烦恼。不管是经别人传授而掌握知识，还是经自己勤学而掌握知识，都不能说有了真智慧。什么是真智慧呢？即要明白可与不可都一样的

道理。至人无智、无德、无功、无名，没有人知道他，也没有人替他传名于后世。这样的人，并不是有意要变得大智若愚，而是已经超越贤与愚、得与失的区分，达到了更高的境界。

追逐世间浮名与虚利的痴愚之人，大略就有以上几类。实质世上万事皆非，没必要在意，也不值得期盼。

*

因幡国有位入道的女儿容貌非凡，来求婚的人极多。但这女子平常只吃栗子，不进米面，其父就对求婚的众人说：“我这女儿，不是寻常之人，不可以与人婚配。”就这样把前来求婚的人都回绝了。

*

五月初五，驱车去贺茂神社观看赛马，到后，发现围观的人极多，车上无法观看，就下了车，想到马场的围栏边去近看。然而那里更为拥挤，根本无法靠近。

这时发现对面一棵楝树上，有个法师蹲踞在树杈中

间，手扶着身旁的树枝打瞌睡。每当眼看就要掉下来时，就会惊醒过来，如此反复再三。观众中有人嘲讽说：“真是个大蠢物，在这么高的树枝上还能安心睡觉？”

我听了这话，心中忽然有所触动，便应声道：“我等又怎知死期不近在眼前呢？还不是整天在这儿观看赛马，比那法师，岂不更蠢？”

众人闻言，都回头看着我，点头说：“足下所言极是，此事确实愚蠢。”于是一边说“请进、请进”，一边为我让开一席之地，使我得以近前。

其实这道理人人都知道，只不过在这种场合下，犹如现场说法，让人听了更有当头一棒、恍然大悟之感。人非木石，触景生情是情理之中的事。

*

有志于出家参悟佛乘、圆满功德的人，心中纵有万千难以舍弃、不能心安之事，也要当即放下。有人或者会想：“这件事随手就可以办了”，“那件事也随手就能办妥”，“这些事，为了不给将来留下麻烦，也免得让人嘲笑，还是先处理妥当为好”，“这么多年都忙碌过来了，

这点事也不太费时间，还是不急这一时片刻吧”。如果这样，则无可逃避的事反而会越来越多，无穷无尽，最终永无修行之日。

世间略有慧根而有心向佛的人不少，但都耽误在这样的想法中，枉度了一生。遇到火灾要逃命时，哪有说“再等一等”的道理？为了保住性命，总会顾不上羞耻，抛下家中财物就跑。生命的迫促，也像大火一样不会等人。无常相逼，比水火之灾还要紧迫，也更难逃脱。死期一到，家中的老人、幼子，身受的君恩、人情，一切难舍之人事，也都不得不舍弃了。

*

书写上人，即因长诵《法华经》而臻于六根清净之境的法师。

某日，上人在旅舍进房之际，听到用豆荚煮豆时发出的咕嘟咕嘟之声，似是豆子在对豆荚说：“君等是我近亲，为何如此无情地煮我，让我痛苦难当？”豆荚的毕剥爆裂之声，似又在回答说：“这不是我等的本意，我等被烧，也已不堪忍受其苦，实在无能为力啊！求你不要出语抱怨了。”

*

听到一个人的名字，心中就在想象其相貌，待见面之后，才发现与之前的想象完全不同。

听到过去的掌故，则容易联想到今日的某户人家，且也将今日之人物，与昔日之人物相比较。这些都是人之常情，不独我如此。

又有时候，眼前的所闻所见，让自己觉得过去某个时候也同样经历过，虽然记不起确切时间，但肯定确有其事。这种感觉，恐怕也不是我才有的吧?

*

没品位的事有：坐席四周常用之物多；砚上笔多；佛堂内佛像多；庭院草木山石多；家中子孙多；与人见面话多；祈愿文中自述的善行多。

虽多而百看不厌的什物有：文车上的书卷；尘冢上的积尘。

*

我不知道人为何要为无聊所苦。不要用心于外物，最好的办法，是一个人独处。

一旦把心放在世俗，就免不了被它迷惑，失去自主。比如和别人交谈，总想博得别人的好感，就做不到言为心声了。又不免有和人嬉闹的时候，有和人争执的时候，以至于喜怒不定，妄念丛生，得失之心就再难放下。

如此执迷于尘世，陶醉其中，且又好发痴心梦想，全不悟我佛真谛。就算无法彻悟佛理，只要能了断俗缘，让此身清净，澄清俗务，让此心安宁，也还可以暂得此生之乐。生活、人事、技艺、学问诸般，都得放下，《摩诃止观》如是说。

*

有世上盛传的事，非当事之人，却知之甚详，一边与人说，一边向人打听，好不奇怪。偏远地区的和尚们尤其有此嗜好，尽皆热衷于打听俗事，好像是自己的事一样，然后滔滔不绝地说与他人听，真不知其何以知道

得如此详尽!

*

对俗世盛传的奇闻异事津津乐道，实在是无聊。也有种人，当事情已流传很久了，他还懵然不知，是为清雅之人也。彼此熟稔的人之间经常谈论的话题、物事，只消片言只语，便能相互会意。

初来乍到者，则不知其所云，遂有身在局外之窘。此种情况，未免于人情世故有所不合，而品流低下的人必犯此病。

*

有人说:“书籍墨宝用薄绢装裱，容易损坏，真是没有办法。”顿阿听了说:“薄绢装裱的东西，两端有所破损，或其螺钿卷轴上的贝壳有所脱落，都是可喜的事。”真是超人一等的见识。又有人说，一部草子中的各册装帧不统一，看着令人极不舒服。弘融僧都却说:“把什么都弄得整齐划一，是无聊人才会做的事。就要参差残缺

才好。”这话也品之有味。

把什么都弄得规整如一，确实令人难以忍受。没有完成的东西，保持其没有完成的样子，不仅别具趣味，还有意犹未尽之妙。又有人说：“建造皇宫时必定会留下若干未曾完成的地方。”

先贤所著的内外典籍中，也有不少残章断文。

*

大纳言法印有一童仆，名叫乙鹤丸，常与某贵人相往来。

有天，乙鹤丸从那贵人处回来，法印问：“到哪里去了？”童仆答：“去某贵人家了。”“他是俗家人还是出家人？”

童仆两袖拢在胸前期期艾艾地说：“不……不太清楚，没见到他的头顶。”

不过，我倒想知道——为什么他不提议看看贵人身体的其他部分呢？[1]

---

1. 此处微妙暗示了男色关系。日本自古以来男色文化兴盛，尤以稚子受人欢迎。——译者注

*

关于赤舌日的诸种说法，阴阳道未曾提及。古人于此并不忌讳，近来有人说起，才讲究起来。民间的说法是：此日百事不顺。做事都不能圆满，到手之物也会放脱，有什么谋划都要落空。如此等等都是愚昧无知的迷信。在吉日里办的事，其顺利的和不顺利的，数量其实大致相当。

原因在于，世间本是变化无常的所在，各种可能都存在。人一旦开始做某事，就对结果满心期待。但人心是变幻不定的，事物的结果也因而不能确定，随时都在随人心而变化。这个道理，常人都不明白。古人云，吉日为恶必凶，凶日行善必吉，吉凶皆由人定，而非由日期定。

*

有人初学射箭，就一次拿上两支箭瞄准箭靶。

师父说：“初学者不要一次拿两支箭。想到后面还有一箭的机会，对第一箭，就不会用全心。射箭时心中不能患得患失，要专注于这一箭，而且要志在必得。”师父

当前，就算只发两箭，也不能忽略其中之一。这中间的懈怠之心，自己可能并未意识到，但师父却能洞察。同样的道理，可以用在其他事情上。

学道之人，晚上惦记着明早的功课，早晨又惦记着当晚的功课，看起来是日催一日，勤奋精进，但其间有刹那的懈怠之心，自己恐怕是没有察觉的吧？为何只专注于当前的一念一世，就这么难呢？

*

有人在闲聊中说：“有个买牛的人，与卖牛的人说好明日付钱后就把牛牵走，不料当晚牛就死了。这样的事，对买者有利，对卖者则是损失。”

旁边有人听了说：“牛主人确实有损失，但未必没有大利。具体说来，生者是料想不到死期逼近的，牛如此，人也如此。牛的死，是意料之外的事；牛主人的生死，恐怕一样难料，但与牛相比，已多得一日之生。一日的生命，值过万金，一头牛的价钱与之相比，简直轻如鸿毛。所以损失一钱而得到万金，谈不上什么损失吧？”

众人听了都嘲笑他说：“这道理怕不仅适用于牛主

人吧！”

那人又说:“怕死的话，就该爱惜生命，故理当日日享受生之愉悦。但愚驽之人忘了生命本身的愉悦，不辞劳苦地追逐身外之乐；忘了生命本身即财宝，而不顾生死地贪求身外之财，从不满足。既不知生的乐趣，又害怕死的到来，这两种情况是不会并存的。人活得不快乐，恰恰是因为不怕死；人不是不怕死，而是忘记了死就是眼前的事。只有超越了死生，才算得参透真谛。”

听了这段宏论，众人益发嘲笑他了。

*

有个女子，幽居在荒僻无人的地方，也不知是在逃避什么。某傍晚时分，月色朦胧之际，一名男子悄然来访，惹得犬儿汪汪地叫起来，侍女出门探视，问:“是何方的贵客呢？”乃把他引入院中。

见到一派凄凉景象，他不由得心中黯然，寻思道:此地岂宜佳人久居？随后在屋前粗陋的木板上立候了片刻，听得里面一个恬静稚细的声音传来:“请进吧！”才拉开已不灵便的门走进去。

室内的情形，却不似外面那么荒凉，别有一番幽雅景致。炉火摇曳，微光影绰，四壁之物皆因之熠熠生辉；暗盈的薰香，却不是为来客新燃起的，闻着倍觉亲切。

又听女主人说："烦请将门关好，怕是要下雨了。车可停于门下，诸随从的住宿也请妥善安排。"随从皆嗡嗡窃语道："到。"

于是相对絮语，把近况一一说与她听。不知不觉间，就听到了第一声鸡鸣，但意兴仍然浓厚，继续倾心交谈，于过去、未来莫不畅所欲言。不久，又听到雄鸡高唱，想必天亮了吧？不过此地是僻静之所，不必如别处需趁暗夜匆匆离去。所以等亮光已从门隙间透入时，才从容起身辞别。

出来时已是四月初夏的曙色，树梢与庭草都深翠欲滴，景色绝美。登车之后，一夜的深情相晤，还萦回于心，恋恋不舍中，回首门前之大桂树，一直到车儿渐行渐远，再看不到为止。

*

一位攀树的名手叫某人到树的高处去砍伐树枝，当

攀树的人爬到很高的地方时，他在下面一言不发；当攀树的人下到如屋檐高的地方时，他才说："小心点，别掉下来了。"

我好奇地问他："已到此处，一跃而下都无妨，为何还提醒他呢？"

他回答说："恰好要在此处提醒呢。人到了高处，会感觉头晕目眩，看着又高又细的树条，自己都会警惕起来，所以不需要提醒。但失误多出现在感觉轻松的地方，所以必须提醒他。"

虽然是身份卑微之人，说出的道理，却颇合乎圣人的训诫。

蹴鞠也是同样的道理，把高难度的动作对付了，如果掉以轻心，球则必然掉在地上。

*

不宜结交为友的人有：一、地位尊贵的人；二、年纪太轻的人；三、健壮无病的人；四、嗜酒的人；五、勇武暴躁的人；六、爱说谎的人；七、贪欲太盛的人。

可结为良友的人有：一、乐善好施的人；二、医师；

三、有慧根灵性的人。

*

人常饲养的家畜是马与牛，套上枷辕后，终日奴役，实在可叹。然而马与牛又是日常不可或缺的东西，莫奈何也。狗能够守夜防盗，比人还能干，也是不可或缺的，故每家都养，但不必搜求更多来喂养。

其余各种鸟兽就没有什么实际用途了。把走兽带回家中，锁上铁链，把飞鸟剪掉羽毛，放进鸟笼，让它们那思恋云霄、怀想山野的愁苦永无尽头，如果换作人，恐怕也难忍受吧？所以有心之人，怎能以此为乐呢？残害生灵来娱乐自己的人，其心与桀纣何异？

王子猷爱鸟，称林中嬉戏的鸟儿为逍遥之友。他不会把鸟儿捉回家让它痛苦的。《尚书》云：“珍禽奇兽不育于国。”

*

雅房大纳言才学俱佳，品行高卓，皇上准备升任他

为大将军，但身边的近臣却说：“最近看到些见不得人的事。”

皇上问：“什么事呢？”回答说：“我从墙壁的缝隙间，看见雅房卿割下活犬的脚来喂鹰。”

皇上听了心中大为厌恶，对雅房的印象顿时改变，升迁之事也就搁置了。

其实犬足饲鹰等等，全属乌有之事。遭人诽谤，固然不幸，但君王听说有这种事，心生憎恶之情，其仁爱之心也甚为感人。

总而言之，以杀戮、折磨动物为乐的人，就像以自相残杀为乐的牲畜。上自鸟兽，下至昆虫，如果细心观察它们的行为的话，就看得出它们也爱护幼子、关怀亲人，有夫有妻，会嫉妒、会发火，有七情六欲，也爱惜生命，甚至比人还执迷痴愚。折磨它们的身体、夺去它们的生命，实在令人痛心。对世间一切众生不怀慈悲之心者，不能视之为人。

*

颜回的志向是不将自己的意志强加于人。大体说来，

残虐生灵之事不可为，贱民的意志，也不能剥夺。

有人喜欢用谎话来哄骗、恫吓和戏谑幼童，这些谎话，在成人看来，也许并不觉得有什么，但对幼童的心灵，则有深刻的影响。他们会感到恐惧、羞耻、悲痛，好像亲身经历了那样的事一样。用别人的痛苦来让自己开心的人，是没有慈悲之心的人。

成人的喜怒哀乐都是心中的虚妄，但人都当作实有之相来在意。

伤害心灵，比伤害身体更为严重。病痛多半来自心中，少有来自外界。服药发汗，有时会没有效果；而心中羞愧恐惧时，则必定要出汗。由此可见心的作用，书凌云之额而忽然白头的典故，即是先例。

*

盛开的樱花和明朗的月色，世人所能观赏的，难道仅此二者？不论对阴雨而怀明月，抑或垂帘幽居不问春归何处，都是极有情趣的事。而如含苞待放的树梢、落花遍地的庭院等等，可供观赏之处还多着呢。和歌之小序中有“本要看花而花已零落”或“无奈没能前去赏花”

的话，其难道不比“赏着了花”之类更有味吗？花殒月沉，皆为之惋惜嗟叹，这是人之常情，但只有俗不可耐的人才说得出这样的话：“这儿的花没了，那儿的花也没了，没什么看头了！”

世上的事，最令人回味的，是始和终这两端。男女恋爱，也是如此。恋爱之真味，不只在于日日相会长相厮守。有时要因暂难相会而忧虑重重，有时要悲叹缘分之变幻莫测，有时独自辗转到天明，有时遥寄相思于远地，有时则远避他乡而追怀往日，凡此种种，都体验过了，才敢说明白了恋爱的真谛。

发皎洁之光而令人一望千里的满月，不如期盼了一夜，到天快亮时才姗姗而来的月有意味。此时的月，略带青苍之色，或在远山之杉树梢间隐现，或为天上之雨云遮断，都极其有味。一丛丛的椎木与白橡树，叶面如洗，辉映在月光下，望之沁人心脾。此情此景，岂能无会心者共赏？不禁怀想起京中的诸友来。

大体说来，可观赏者，岂只限于眼前所见之月与花？春日闭门家中，或月夜静处室内时，于心中想象其风致，也别有兴味。

品流高尚的人物虽好物而不溺于物，虽兴致颇高

也能淡然处之。只有那些不解风雅的村夫俗子，才于游赏时力求尽兴。赏花时拥挤在花下，或凑近盯着花看，要饮酒，要作连歌，末了手持折下的花枝，欢欢喜喜地打道回府；路过泉水时，一定要把手足都泡进去；遇到下雪时，一定要在雪地上踩踏，留下自己的足印。总之凡有景致处，决不悠然旁观，一定要去耍弄一番才甘心。

此辈观看贺茂祭的情形，也是妙不可言。“祭神的行列要有一阵才过来呢，这会儿待在看台上有什么意思？”说罢就拥入看台后的人家里，饮酒、大嚼，下围棋、双六。待到外面放风之人喊道“行列过来了！”才又一拥而出，你推我搡地挤上看台，连看台上的布帘也似要被其挤落了。在观看时，此辈绝不错过任何细节，且都要评头论足一番。当一个行列过去后，就说：“咱回去等下一轮吧。”又钻回台后的屋子去戏耍了。此辈人眼中，只认实在之物。

比较起来，京都人士就要文雅得多。彼等做闭目养神状，似乎并不热衷于观看。职位较低的年轻侍从们紧随其主，立于身后，也没有谁探身引颈做粗俗状。总之这群人中，没有一个表现出一定要看个清楚才甘心的样子。

现场到处悬挂着葵叶，秀雅可人，而驾车前来者，已在天色未明之际悄然云集于此，车中人不时左右探望，看看有无旧识，打打招呼。众车错杂相陈，有的妙趣横生，有的光彩夺目，颇富观赏趣味，在等待时，细加观玩，倒颇能解闷。然而到了日暮时分，一排排牛车与拥挤不堪的人群便突然不知去向，变得稀疏零落，看台上的布帘与坐垫也纷纷被取走了，眼前呈现一片凄凉景象，让人联想到世道的盛衰，不禁感慨有加。把大路上的情景，这样看下来，才可以说观了贺茂祭。

聚集于看台之上的众人中，相识的人不少，可知世上的人，其实并不太多。假设我须等到众人死后才最后死去，实在也等不了太久。在一个大容器中盛满水，在它的底部凿开一个小孔，水于是要往下流。这孔虽然细小，但如果长流不止，也不需要太久，水就会流尽。京都的人虽多，但每日都有人死去，且不止一二人。鸟部野、舟冈及众多无名野山上，只见过送葬之人众多的时候，没见过无人前去送葬的时候。因此卖棺材者的棺材做好不久就能卖出，不论老幼强弱，皆死期难料，侥幸能活到今天，实在是不可思议的奇妙之事。所以人生在世，来日方长的想法，是片刻都不能有的。

可尝试将双六的棋子排作“继子立”的形状，当其首尾成列之后，起初不知从何处下手取子。等数下数来，则依数取出一子；其他诸子，似乎还安然无事；然而再数、再取，最终会一子不剩。人死也是如此：死是必然的，所不同者先后而已。战士在阵前，知道死亡就在眼前，所以能身家两忘，不顾一切。遁世之人长住茅庵，静享林泉之趣，如果自以为与战士阵前迥乎不同，那就太不明智了。深山里虽然静僻，难道“无常”这个敌人就不会挟常胜之势来攻打你？此时与死面对，与战士在战场上的情形，并无不同。

*

留下身后之财，是智者不为的事。积蓄不好的东西没有意义，而好东西再舍不得也终不能带走。一生积蓄太多，反而是件苦事。口称“我一定要得到它”，而争夺人死后遗物的行径，尤其丑恶。凡想于身后留给某人的东西，最好在世的时候就给他。

人除了日常必需品外，别的东西就不用再有了。

*

看起来毫无情趣的人，只言片语中，偶尔也有可取之处。

有个乡村武士，凶神恶煞的样子，有次问旁边的人：“你有子女吗？”那人回答说：“一个也没有。”

武士就说：“没有子女的人是不懂人间真情的。如此说来，你真是个冷酷无情的人，可怕呀！”

这可谓至理名言。不懂恩爱的人，心中就没有慈悲之心。不懂得孝养的人，有了子女后，才会明白父母之心。

舍世出家的人，孑然一身，与万事不相关联，常常鄙视羁绊尘世、谄人媚上、欲望深重的人，其实也不应当。若换了自己，为了至爱的亲人与妻儿，就算不顾廉耻地沦为盗贼，也必然会愿意的。缉拿盗贼，因他所犯的恶行而治他的罪，不如把国家治理好，让世人免于饥寒。人无恒产，则无恒心，人穷则为盗，如果国家治理不善，人民会受饥寒之苦，犯罪之人也难以绝迹。把人置于苦难之中，使其犯法，又绳之以法，真是可悲的做法。

然而如何才能普惠众生呢？上能摒弃奢靡，下能抚

民劝农，则天下必得其利。倘有人在衣食能保的情况下，还要为非作恶，那就是真正的盗贼了。

*

御随身秦重躬在谈到北面武士下野入道信愿时，说：“这人是落马之相，当慎之又慎！”但信愿一向不以此为然，最后果然落马而亡。秦重躬真是精于此道的人，一句话，就让人视之为神人。

后来有人请教他：“什么叫作落马之相呢？”他回答说：“此人的臀部状似桃核，又好骑沛艾之马，故有落马之相。看来我这话，是说中了。”

*

没什么要紧的事，到别人家里去盘桓，是不好的。最好有事才去，事了之后就回来。在别人家中待得太久，也特别让人讨厌。

坐在一起后，话必定就多，令人身体疲惫，心中烦乱，既耽误做事，又浪费时间，于人于己都无益处。对

客人感厌烦时，也不宜说话烦躁。如果不喜欢来客久坐，就明白地告诉他也无妨。

至于情趣相投，愿意畅谈的人，如果正好无事可忙，就可以说：“请不妨安坐，今日可以做一长谈。”阮籍的青眼、白眼，恐怕人人都有吧。

如果没什么事，过来坐坐，悠然闲谈一阵，然后回去，也不错。或者修书一封，说“久未奉教”云云，也颇为愉快。

*

少年时血气旺盛，心易动，多情欲，此时恰如落地而走的珍珠，容易触物而碎，常有性命之危。年少的时候，总会做一些耽误自己的事：或者贪好美艳之物而不惜钱财；或者心血来潮舍红尘而着僧衣；或者逞强斗狠，既耻于不如人，又羡慕别人比自己强，喜好多变，每日不同；或者沉溺女色，感情用事，讲究仗义而误了大事；或者竟然效仿他人而不惜一死，从不知爱惜生命以求长寿；又或者因好色之名而饱受物议。

老年人精神衰退，嗜欲清淡，对于外物，能够无动

于衷，心中自然平静，不会做无益之事，要爱惜身体，既不自烦，也不扰人。年老后，智慧胜过年轻时，就好比年轻时容貌风采胜过老年。

*

世上有许多不可思议的事。

但凡有事，一定要喝酒，且喜欢强行劝酒，真不知道理何在。被劝酒的人，端着酒杯，皱着眉头，一脸为难之色，直想趁人不备扔下酒杯逃走。然而被发现后，则牵裳捉臂地被留在座上，强行灌饮。结果本来稳重端庄的人，变得疯疯癫癫，一味丢人现眼；本来正常的人，变成病重的人，醉得分不清前后左右，倒头便睡。这样的事如果发生在喜庆的场合，更是令人咂舌。大醉的次日醒来，头痛欲裂，粒米难进，躺在床上痛苦呻吟，昨日的事仿佛发生在前世，一点也记不得了。公私大事都被耽误，造成诸多不便。让人落到这地步的人，既不仁，也无礼；而遭此不幸的人，对强行灌酒的人，又岂能不心生怨恨？假如这样的陋习，只在外国有，而我国没有，我们听起来，一定会觉得匪夷所思吧。

酒席上的众生相，若只是旁观，也会觉得不堪入目：体面而有教养的人，在酒席上却放肆笑骂，说起话来喋喋不休，乌帽歪着，上衣敞着，下装高卷，双腿裸裎，全然不顾体统，与平时的举止大相径庭；女人则撩起头发，不知羞耻地媚笑撒娇，掰开那端着酒的粗人的嘴巴，往里面塞进菜肴，自己也大嚼不已，真是丑态难当；一众人尽力吼叫着，自歌自舞，甚至叫来年长的法师，光着污黑的臂膀，一副不堪入目的恶俗样，连兴致勃勃的旁观者都觉得再也看不下去。

有人喝醉了喜欢夸夸其谈，吹嘘自己，还强迫身边的人洗耳恭听；有人喝醉了就哭泣；贱人们则相互谩骂，大打出手，让人既惊又怕。接下来就开始为非作歹，强取别人之物，或摔倒在屋檐下，或自马及车上坠落受伤。无车可乘的人，就跌跌撞撞地走在大路上，到土墙下或别人门前去行那方便之事。还有身着袈裟的年长法师，扶着小童的肩，满口胡言、步履蹒跚，看着让人心生怜悯。

如此等等，倘有益于今生来世，倒也无话可说；但实际而言，酒之于今生，是令人犯错误、损财货、生疾病之物。虽然号称“百药之长”，但百病皆因酒而生；虽

然号称可以解忧，但醉后反易让人伤心而泣。于来世而言，酒让人丧失心智，如被火烧去善根，恶胆顿生，破除诸戒，最终必堕入地狱。佛祖云："若以己手持酒器与人饮者，五百世轮回中无手。"

然而酒虽有如上可厌处，也有其可爱而难舍时。月之夜、雪之朝、花之下，与人悠然闲谈，举杯小饮，可以助清兴，发雅趣；闲暇之日，友人意外来访，则端出酒食，小加款待，心情也甚为愉快。在高贵之人家里，酒食出于庖厨，经美人之手端来席上，感觉也颇不错。

隆冬之日，斗室之中，于火上小煮点什么，与亲密知己举杯豪饮，是极有味的事。在旅舍或山野间，口中说着"何不上酒肴"，而径直在草地上坐下饮用，也有意趣。不善饮者，为人所强劝，则少许饮下一点，是不错的事。此时座中有身份的人端起酒杯自言自语："那么我就再来一杯如何？反正酒已不多了。"听着令人高兴。若自己酒量甚豪，席上又有极愿结识的人在，则与之杯盏相亲，也是十分可喜的事。

善饮的人，其实也天真可爱，颇为有趣。在别人家中醉卧不起，早上，主人家拉开纸窗时，他顿时手脚慌乱，睡眼惺忪，细髻曝露，都来不及穿衣，一把抱在手

上就狼狈而逃。看着他穿着短衣短裤的背影和长满毛发的瘦腿，实在是有趣，还真像个醉汉的模样。

*

男子不应有妻。

我每听人说“我一向独居”，就觉得其人不俗；听说其为某人女婿或要带回某女同住，就极其反感。我猜想，那人其实没什么头脑，竟把平常女子认作美人，一定要迎娶回家。如果女子确实是美人，则那人必定全心全意地侍奉着，就像我侍奉佛祖一样。我这想法大体是没有错的。主持家政的女人尤其让人讨厌，生儿育女，百般宠爱，也是毫无意义的事。男人死后，女人削发为尼，其年老之丑状，就算男人死了，也很难让人接受。

不管是何种女人，与她相处久了，也会心生厌恶。从女方看来，不谈婚娶，就有悬空而无着落之感。但不同住而经常往来的男女，反而可能成为感情持久、至死不渝的伴侣。不期然而来，留宿一夜，可于双方都保有新鲜之感。

*

所谓入夜则无物可观的说法，是不足取的。

万物的光华、装饰与色彩，在夜晚看来更觉不同凡响。白天的装束可以简淡朴素一点，到了晚上，则以绚丽华美为佳。灯光之下，人的容颜神采看上去会美上加美。别人的谈话，在暗处听来，也更觉优雅而有味。各种香味与音乐，都在夜晚更加动人。

平时有夜深来访之人，觉得别有一番清新韵致，颇为有味。青年人无时不在打量着他人的装束容貌，特别在可以放任的场合，不分便装与盛装，都是用心打扮了的。美男子在日暮时分才开始梳头，女子也是在夜色渐深的时候才离开座位，拿出镜子来化妆。这些都很有味道。

*

德大寺右大臣大人任检非违使的时候，有一日在中门使厅讨论官厅公事，官人章兼牛车上的牛走脱了，来到使厅，径直走上大理所坐的滨床，卧床反刍。这是少有的怪事，众人都说应该把牛牵到阴阳师那里断一断吉凶。

大理之父相国说：“牛又不晓得人事，既然有脚，哪里不能去？因为这点意外就要没收小吏的牛，真是岂有此理！”于是将牛归还其主人，更换掉卧席，此后并无不吉利之事发生。

这正是“见怪不怪，其怪自败”。

*

世事无常，万物都不足以长久倚赖。执迷不悟的人深信此生有物可恃，必争为己有，于是心生怨怒之情。

实则权势不可倚赖，因为强者先亡；财富不可倚赖，因为可以轻易散尽；才学不可倚赖，因为孔子也有怀才不遇的时候；德行不可倚赖，因为颜回也是不幸之人；君王的宠幸不可倚赖，因为说不准何时会有杀身之祸；奴仆的恭顺不可倚赖，因为难免有叛逃的事发生；人的志向不可倚赖，因为志向总有变化的时候；说好的事，不可倚赖，因为守信的人太少。

既然自己与他人都不可靠，那么时运来时固然可喜，时运背时也不要抱怨。左右广大才无障碍，前后远阔方能通畅。若置身于逼仄处，则容易有冲突毁损；若用心

于狭隘处，则不能舒坦通泰；拂逆他人而与之相争，则容易伤及身体。若能心宽而性柔，才可以毫发无损。

人为天地灵长，天地无限，人之心性也一样。人心如能广大无垠，则不为喜怒所羁绊，也不为外物所烦扰。

*

丹波有个地方叫出云，有个大神社迁移来此，建筑极为雄伟。此地是名为志太的人的任职之地，到了秋天，这个志太就邀请圣海上人等一众人，说：“敬请光临出云之神社，将以萩饼款待诸君。”于是带着众人来到了神社。众人于社中各处参拜，深为震服，无不肃然起敬。

神社前有一狮子和一狛犬之石像，二者相背而立。上人看了极为感动，含着眼泪说：“善哉善哉，这狮犬的立向，实为罕见，必有其深意在，诸君若不留意此稀有之景，实在可惜！”

众人也觉得奇怪，都说：“确实和别的地方不同，回去后一定要把这地方的胜景告诉都中人士。”

上人还想追究它的来由，就叫来一位看着体体面面、博学多闻的神官，问道：“贵社的狮子如此安放，是有什

么来由的吧？愿闻其详。”

神官回答说：“这实在是顽童所为，真是岂有此理！”于是上前将狮子与狛犬的方向调回到正面相对的原状。

上人的感动之泪，算是白流了。

*

男女之于暗夜私会，既怕人见到，又怕人听到，但心中恋情之强烈，不见不行。此种情形于日后必然永难忘怀。如是那种经父母兄弟同意了的明媒正娶，就让人扫兴得很了。

有迫于生计的女子，因贪慕钱财，就托人对根本不相配的老法师或乡巴佬说：“愿奉君之箕帚。”媒人也两头说好话，尽力撮合，于是把这素不相识的女子迎娶回来。这真是难以接受的事。这样的夫妇之间，有什么话可说呢？夫妇之间，能够一起回忆当年恋爱如何辛苦，如何担惊受怕地只求一见的情形，那才叫情深意永呢。

凡是由他人撮合的夫妇，不免会厌恶对方，常常闹得不愉快。若本是品貌俱无的老朽，把年轻貌美的女子娶回来，想着这么个美女竟下嫁我这副德行的人，心中

恐怕也会不太自在吧？品貌都不如人，相比之下，必定会自惭形秽，这样过着真没什么意思。

梅香暗吐、月色朦胧之夜，伫立在她身旁；或任由宅垣旁的草露沾湿了衣裳，和她一起踏着晓月回去——没有这些可供追忆的往事，还不如不要谈情说爱。

*

十五的满月瞬间即亏，不留心观察的人是看不到月在一夜中的变化的。

人在重病之时，病况也是时刻都在变化，不觉就濒于死亡。

当病情还不至于致命，就习惯性地想着存世之日还长久，还可以完成若干心愿，然后再潜心修佛；当病情加重，快迈进鬼门关时，自己还一事无成，才后悔一向的懈怠，想着这次若能痊愈，保住一命，一定要夜以继日、勇猛精进，完成这件事、那件事；虽然发了这些誓，但病情突然恶化，神志不清，行为失控，最终还是过世了。世上的人，以这样的人居多。所以最紧要而需要牢记的事是：

人都想完成了各种心愿后，再把余下的时间用以事佛，但人的心愿是无穷无尽的。在变幻莫测的一生中，能做成什么事呢？一切愿望都是妄想。愿望的产生，源于心的迷乱，所以一桩也不要去做了。要立即放下一切，一心向佛，心中才坦然无碍；只有一无所为，才能保全身心的宁静。

*

我八岁的时候曾问家父："什么是佛？"

家父回答："佛是人所化。"

我又问："人怎么才能化为佛呢？"

家父又回答说："遵从佛的教诲就可以成佛。"

我又问："教人的佛，又是谁教的呢？"

家父又回答说："是他之前的佛教的。"

我又问："那么第一个教人成佛的佛是什么样的呢？"

家父大笑着说："要不是从天上掉下来的，就是从地里冒出来的，谁知道呢！"

后来家父在与众人笑谈时说："追问到这地步，就实在无法回答了。"

企鹅经典：小黑书　第一辑

01.　贝尔科洛蕾夫人与神父

[意] 薄伽丘

02.　泄密的心

[美] 爱伦·坡

03.　醋栗

[俄] 契诃夫

04.　一个人需要许多土地吗?

[俄] 列夫·托尔斯泰

05.　一颗简单的心

[法] 福楼拜

06.　傻子的一生

[日] 芥川龙之介

07.　萎缩的胳膊

[英] 托马斯·哈代

08.　樱花树下的清酒

[日] 吉田兼好

09.　虎！虎！

[英] 威廉·布莱克

10.　给一个青年诗人的十封信

[奥] 里尔克